PREGNANT BY THE PLAYBOY

FONG BROTHERS, BOOK 1

JACKIE LAU

First edition: May 2020
ISBN: 978-1-989610-11-4

Editor: Latoya C. Smith, LCS Literary Services

Cover Design: Flirtation Designs

Cover photograph: Depositphotos

[1]

VINCE

I'M IN LOVE.

Her name is Evie, short for Evelyn.

She's four and a half months old, and she gives me a gummy smile and laughs whenever I press her nose and say "beep."

Last week, she wasn't amused by this, but today, it's provided endless giggles.

She also enjoys it when I sing, but that's a secret between me and her. Normally, I have no qualms about embarrassing myself —as many people will attest to—but I don't want anyone to know that I sing to my niece.

I visit Evie and Courtney, my sister-in-law, every Friday afternoon, and don't tell anyone this, either, but Friday is now my favorite day of the week. And it has nothing to do with any parties or clubs I might go to late in the evening.

While Courtney has a shower and does laundry, I entertain my niece, and then the three of us hang out together, and Evie naps a bit. I don't know much about babies, but I'm told Evie is a rather easygoing and chill baby. Surprising that my brother Julian produced such a child.

I carry Evie over to the mat in the playroom and sit cross-legged with her in my lap. There's a mirror in front of us, but I doubt she understands that it's her in the mirror.

"Say hello to the baby!" I hold up her little hand and wave. Then I press her nose again. "Beep. Beep, beep."

She giggles. She's so easily amused.

She's wearing a yellow duckie onesie today. Her hair is black and fine, and her eyes are dark. Her ears stick out, just a bit.

When Julian first put Evie in my arms, the day after she was born, I wasn't sure what to do. I'd never held a baby before, and she was so tiny and rather strange-looking, wearing an enormous white knit hat with a bow, her face scrunched up.

Julian took two weeks off work—he's the CEO of Fong Investments—and after he went back to work, he made me promise to visit every week and make sure Courtney and Evie were getting along okay. He was probably also trying to save me from my unfulfilling life of leisure by giving me something productive to do.

I haven't worked in almost three and a half years, though I never need to work again. I have more than enough money after selling my start-up.

My family doesn't realize it—because I was in Silicon Valley for most of that time—but I burnt out *bad*. They think of me as the wild troublemaker, but I did basically nothing but work for five years. Responsible, serious Julian can handle that kind of lifestyle, though even he realized that he had to stop pushing himself quite so hard, but I can't.

I press on Evie's forehead. "Beep."

She frowns at the mirror. *Silly Uncle Vince, don't you know my nose makes noises, not my forehead?*

Perhaps it's time for a song. I start singing her favorite, "There Was an Old Woman Who Swallowed a Fly." I'm on the verse about the goat when I hear a noise behind me, and I freeze.

Courtney picks up Evie. "Uncle Vince was singing to you, wasn't he?"

Evie nods.

The traitor.

"Evie," I say sternly. "That was a secret."

I have a reputation to uphold, and singing to babies doesn't fit it.

Though Courtney knows me pretty well. We've always gotten along, and she's helped me with some things that most people don't know about.

"You want to stay for dinner?" she asks.

"Nah, sorry, I've got plans, but I'll stay until Julian gets back." I lean forward and touch Evie's nose again. "Beeeeeeeep!"

"I got you a present," I say to Julian as soon as he walks in the door and sets down his briefcase. "You'll *love* it."

"Dear God," he mutters. "To what do I owe this pleasure?"

"Just saw something at the store and figured you'd like it," I say cheerfully.

Annoying my older brother is one of life's greatest pleasures.

Courtney comes over with Evie, and Julian gives them both a kiss. Once upon a time, I wouldn't have figured Julian would be a family man, but it seems to suit him. There's an odd feeling in my chest as I look at the three of them together.

Then I say, "Come on, it's in the living room."

Julian walks over to his favorite chair and looks at his gift. It's a large plush animal, eating a bowl of noodles with chopsticks, and I've placed a bottle of Labatt 50 with a large red bow next to it, so it sort of looks like the animal is drinking the beer. I've also tied a red bow around the animal.

Julian picks up the beer. "You're never going to let me live this down, are you?"

My brother is mainly a wine drinker, and he has sophisticated taste in wine. But when it comes to beer, he drinks old man beer, and I find it endlessly amusing.

"And this?" He picks up the stuffed animal. "What is it?"

"I don't know, but it made me think of you."

"Why, may I ask, is that?"

"It's Pusheen!" Courtney exclaims.

"Pusheen?" Julian says.

"A cartoon cat! Isn't she sweet? I love Pusheen!"

Julian smiles affectionately at his wife and daughter, then turns back to me. "You're trying to buy presents for Evie again by pretending they're for me. I told you she doesn't need anything else. She has lots of toys."

I shrug. Busted. "The beer is for you, though."

"Thank you," he says sarcastically.

I take this Pusheen creature from his hands and hold it up to Evie. "What do you think? Do you need more toys?"

She gurgles and reaches out to touch the cat.

"I'll take that as a yes," I say.

"You need something to do in life other than spoil my daughter," Julian says.

"Ah, that reminds me. I should head out—I have an orgy to attend."

Courtney makes a show of covering Evie's ears, then hands her over to her father. Julian grins as he bounces her up and down, and she slaps her slobbery hand across his face.

I'm lying—there isn't an orgy tonight. Just a big, fancy party at Brian Poon's. There will likely be some sex, though. There usually is. And I've had a dry spell of…well, six weeks, which is rather long for me.

I just like saying "orgy" to bug Julian.

To be honest, I do tend to exaggerate my exploits a teeny-tiny bit.

Well, it's more than a teeny-tiny bit lately. The first year or so after selling my company, my life truly was wild. A little too wild.

After years of a ridiculous workload, I was suddenly free and very wealthy, so I was celebrating…but at the same time, I was trying to drown out my overwhelming feelings of misery and loneliness. It didn't quite work.

In fact, it was the start of a depressive episode.

But most people don't know about that.

I'm simply Vince Fong, Playboy Extraordinaire. I can't lie; I enjoy people seeing me this way, and it isn't entirely an act.

I like women and sex. Good food and wine. Traveling. Partying.

It's not an everyday occurrence anymore, but it's a good life.

Yet, although I'm feeling better these days, there's still something missing…

"Hello!" says a voice from elsewhere in the house.

"Oh, sorry," Courtney says to Julian. "I forgot to tell you. Your parents and grandmother insisted on coming over for dinner today. They're bringing food, don't worry."

My brother frowns. I think he wanted a quiet night with his wife and daughter.

I saunter to the front hall, Julian and Courtney behind me. "Hey, Mom and Dad. Po Po."

"Vince!" Po Po sits down on the bench to take off her shoes. "You are joining us for dinner?"

"Sorry, I've got plans." Might as well make my exit now. It's six thirty, and I plan to be at Brian's around eight. The party won't start until later, but I enjoy hanging out with Brian.

"It's Friday night," Julian says. "Of course Vince has plans."

Po Po shakes her head and touches Evie's chin. "You be a good girl when you grow up, okay? Not at all like Uncle Vince."

I press my niece's nose. "Beep. Beep. Beep."

"Why are you pretending my daughter is a truck backing up?" Julian asks.

"She likes it," I say.

Of course, this is the one time Evie doesn't giggle.

I try again.

She still doesn't giggle.

I guess I'll have to find something new to entertain her next week.

~

I regard myself in the mirror. I'm wearing a black suit and white shirt. Collar open, no tie. My hair is a little long, in a way that I think really works for me. I smile and point my finger at the mirror.

Yeah, I look the part.

But what's the meaning of a life spent partying and playing videogames and dining in style?

Fuck it.

I'm going to bury myself in a woman tonight and forget about everything.

That's what I need.

[2]

MARISSA

My mouth falls open.

"Your friend lives *here*?" I ask Carrie Lo as our Uber heads through the wrought-iron gates of a house on the Bridle Path.

She shrugs. "Yeah."

"What does Brian do?"

"Nothing."

"What do you mean he does nothing?"

"His family owns a big multinational company," Carrie says. "I think he's involved, but not heavily."

Right.

This is so not my world. I've never been to a house on the Bridle Path before, and it's a freaking monster of a house, with a huge fountain out front. Not that there's any water in it since it's January. A light dusting of snow covers the ground.

I grew up in a two-bedroom apartment in Scarborough. It was just me and my mother, who worked at a dry cleaners. Whenever my mother bought a box of Peek Freans—that was what luxury meant to me. I wouldn't have even been able to conceive of something like this. A house in Toronto with an actual gate and semi-circular driveway.

But I'm thirty-six now, and I don't have to count my nickels to buy a box of cookies. I have a condo and a good job as an engineer.

At the thought of my job, I remember all the shit I have to do on Monday morning.

I push that aside. Tonight, I'm going to have fun. I deserve it.

I've known most of my friends since high school or university, but I only met Carrie a few years ago. She's four years younger than me, and she's all about going out and having fun. Since many of my friends now have children and aren't usually available on Friday nights, it's good to have a friend like Carrie. She works in advertising, although she never seems to do much work, and she's always up-to-date on the hot new places to eat and drink. She's the youngest child in a wealthy family from Hong Kong, and she's always seemed worldlier than me.

I step out of the car in my black boots and long black jacket, and Carrie and I proceed to the door. It's opened by a man who I think might be an honest-to-God butler.

Yeah, this is so not my world.

But I hand him my jacket and take off my boots, and I act like I belong.

I can conquer this party like I've conquered everything else in life.

"I love your dress," Carrie says.

"Thanks." I don't tell her that I found it on a sale rack for a hundred bucks. My outfit is probably worth a tiny fraction of hers. She's wearing a sexy white ruched dress and showy gold jewelry. I feel like her opposite, dressed in black with silver jewelry.

"Brian!" she cries, throwing her arms around an East Asian man in a gray suit. "This is my friend Marissa. The woman I told you about, remember?"

"Nice to meet you," he says, shaking my hand.

We follow him into a room with low lights and loud music. A few people are dancing.

Brian gestures me toward the bar. It's not a help-yourself bar; no, it's staffed by two bartenders. Both Asian men with ponytails and silk jackets that somehow don't look ridiculous.

"I'll have a glass of white wine," I say.

One of them nods, and I turn toward the room as I wait.

Life has been stressful lately. I've been busy with a big project at work, and my mother had a health scare. We got the test results back a few days ago, and fortunately, the tumor is benign.

Now, I finally feel like I can breathe again, and I'm determined to have a good time and maybe end my dry streak. Carrie assured me this would be a good place to get laid.

I feel a touch out of place, but I know I look hot in this outfit, and the key is to be confident.

I also feel a little old. I think most of these people are closer to thirty.

Once the bartender passes over my drink, Carrie grabs my hand and introduces me to a few men she knows. One of them looks at me appreciatively.

"You like him?" Carrie whispers.

I shake my head and grab a petit four off the tray as a waiter passes by.

Carrie knows almost everyone, and she walks me through the gorgeous house, introducing me to men and raising her eyebrows in question. She seems determined to make sure I have sex tonight, and I appreciate it.

We pass a man and woman making out in the hall. The guy's got his tongue down the woman's throat and his hand under her dress. I watch as his hand slides higher…

Many of the men are good-looking, but apparently I'm picky tonight, even if I'm just interested in going to bed, not a relationship. A relationship would be nice, too—I haven't had a boyfriend in two years—but that's not why you go to a party like this.

It's important to do everything with a purpose, and for tonight, mine is simply: have fun and get laid.

And then I see him.

It's like there's a neon arrow above him, pointing down.

He's wearing a black suit and white shirt. He's East Asian, and he has black hair, a little too long to be strictly proper, I think.

He's sitting on a leather couch, next to a woman with red hair and a green dress.

And oh yeah, they're making out.

Yes, the man I've set my sights on is currently making out with another woman. He's got one hand cupping her ass, the other cupping the back of her head, and there's just something about the way he's touching her, molding her body to his. I'm mesmerized.

I want him to do that to me.

Right here, in front of everyone.

My mouth is suddenly dry, and I take a sip of my wine.

"Who's that?" I ask.

"Vince Fong," Carrie replies.

Oh. I swallow.

I know Vince by reputation only. He's the youngest son in the illustrious Fong family. His father started a successful investment company, which his oldest brother now runs. His other brother is a writer. And Vince, he sold his tech start-up for a ton of money a while back, and ever since, he's been rolling in cash and living the high life.

"He's good friends with Brian," Carrie says.

Ah. I can imagine that Brian with his gorgeous house and parties would have a friend like Vince Fong.

As if feeling my gaze on him, Vince breaks the kiss and looks at me.

My instinct is to look away, but no, I'm not going to. I continue to stare.

He winks and shoots me a cocky smile that says he knows exactly what I want. That says he knows he's hot stuff.

These sorts of men usually piss the shit out of me, but for some reason, that smile makes me even more attracted to Vince.

Carrie smirks. "You like him?"

"Yeah," I admit.

"I bet he'd be up for a threesome."

I jolt back.

She laughs. "I'm sure he's had quite a few of those over the years."

But I want Vince all to myself.

He's not the kind of guy I usually like, but I just want someone to show me a great night, and I bet he's more than capable of that.

He presses the redhead against his groin, and I almost gasp, imagining it's me instead of her. She rocks her hips against him, and fuck, I can hear the growl in the back of his throat.

"Marissa Chan," Carrie murmurs. "I've never seen you like this before."

I haven't seen myself like this before, either.

"Alright," she says. "Let's get you what you want."

[3]

VINCE

WHEN ALEXIS GOES to get another drink, the woman in the incredibly sexy black dress struts over to me, one hand on her hip, and it's clear she's a woman on a mission.

I fucking love it.

She's petite, maybe five-two, and rather slight, but she has a huge presence. I've never seen her before—and I'm familiar with most of the people Brian invites to his parties.

She grabs my lapels and tugs me up. Her raised eyebrows indicate a question, and I nod. She can do what she wants to me.

She drags me into the corner, grabs my hand, and puts it on her ass. Oh, wow. And then she stands on her toes and kisses me.

Who *is* this woman?

I had my lips on another woman not a minute ago, but I'm not complaining. I live for shit like this.

Her kiss is a scorcher, and I can't say I'm surprised. Her strokes are quick, then deep and long. She's mixing it up, keeping my head spinning. When I squeeze her ass and press her against my erection, she tears her lips from mine, breathing heavily.

"You want that, baby?" I murmur.

She nods.

I still haven't heard her voice, but fuck, she feels good. I inch up the hem of her dress.

"Yeah?" I say.

She nods again.

I slide my finger over her panties. They're soaked. I push them aside and shove a finger inside her.

Yes. Wet and perfect.

"Vince," she gasps. Her voice is low and throaty and wonderful.

"You know my name." I smile.

"Yeah. I know who you are, Vince Fong."

"Well, that puts me at a disadvantage. I have no idea who you are, even though I have my finger in your pussy."

Her pupils dilate. She loves this.

I'm good at sex because I'm good at reading people. Also, I've had lots of practice.

She starts grinding against my hand, but I don't move, and she moans in frustration.

"Tell me how to get you off," I whisper, my mouth a hair's breadth from her ear. "You want to ride my hand? You want my mouth? What's it take?"

"Your mouth. I want you on your knees."

Oh, hell.

"Tell me what your name is first," I say.

"Marissa."

"You make a habit of kissing men before telling them your name?"

She shakes her head and bites her lip. Just quickly—but it seems to be a nervous gesture. "I've never done this before."

My eyes widen. "You sure acted like you'd done this before."

"No, I just really want you."

Slowly, I slide my finger in and out of her, and she seems utterly entranced.

Not gonna lie, it's damn good for my ego when a woman responds to every little touch and wants me so badly.

That's why I'm a cocky bastard.

"Vince…" she moans.

I pretend to be a little blasé, not wanting her to know quite how much she affects me.

I haven't felt like this in a while.

"Tell me about yourself," I say. "What do you do for a living?"

"I'm a mechanical engineer."

Yeah, this isn't the kind of person who usually shows up at Brian's parties.

"What do you do in your free time?" My finger is still inside her, moisture dripping down my hand.

"Vince," she growls.

It's pretty sexy.

"Favorite movie?" I inquire. "Favorite color? Favorite song? What was the last TV show you binged?"

She gives me a look that says she's totally unimpressed with me.

I laugh.

"Why does any of that matter?" she asks. "I can't think straight enough to answer these goddamn questions when you're touching me."

"I just have a feeling you're one of those people who's really fun to annoy. Seems like I'm right." I kiss her before she can respond, and then I drop to my knees.

Slowly, I slide her panties down her legs. They're red and lacy.

I put them in my pocket.

Then I lift up her skirt, baring her to me—and the rest of the room. Her hair is dark and neatly trimmed. I slide my finger into her again and savor the sight. When I turn my gaze up to her face, she's looking at me with a glazed expression.

"You good?" I say quietly.

"Yeah."

I glance behind me. Alexis has returned, and she's now kissing Carrie Lo on the couch. Brian is standing at the doorway, staring at me and Marissa. He likes to watch, and he's watched me with many women before.

But all I care about is making Marissa feel good and seeing where this will take us. I use my thumbs to spread her open and give her one long, leisurely lick.

Sweet fuck, she tastes amazing.

I swirl my tongue over her clit and she gasps. When I look up, her eyes are shut and her head is tipped back, and I will do whatever it takes for her to continue making those noises.

I lick all over her entrance, then slip my tongue inside her. I thrust my fingers in and out of her at a frantic pace, and her expression is almost one of pain—this is too much for her, she's not used to all this pleasure. But at the same time, she's holding my head against her crotch.

Her body tenses as I continue to fuck her with my fingers, faster and faster. I can tell she's close, so close, and either she wants me so much that she doesn't care if other people can see... or that turns her on, too.

I glance up as her channel clenches around my fingers, and a look of pure ecstasy is written on her face. It makes me so hard as she cries out and trembles.

I pull her down to the ground with me. She's gorgeously disheveled.

And she's giggling. "I can't believe...I did that."

"You're not drunk, are you?" It didn't occur to me before, but now I'm a little worried. It's harder to tell with someone I don't know.

"No, I've only had half a drink. I just feel really good right now. After that orgasm."

I drag her mouth to mine, needing to taste her, maybe needing her to taste herself on my lips, too. "You want to fuck?"

She swallows.

"We can go somewhere more private." I wink. "I know this house well."

"Actually…"

"Or we don't have to do anything else. It's cool."

She strokes my dick through my pants. *Ohhh.*

"Let's leave," she says.

"My place or yours? Or a hotel, if you prefer."

She thinks this over as she straightens her dress. "Your place. We'll get an Uber?"

"Nah, I got a driver out there."

"Of course you do," she murmurs. "Can I have my underwear back?"

I pat my pocket. "Don't see why you'll need them tonight."

"Good point. And by the way, Everclear's 'I Will Buy You a New Life' and *The Great British Bake Off.*" She gets up.

I stay on the floor for another moment, my head spinning.

Right. She just answered two of the inane questions I asked her.

I wasn't planning on leaving the party so early, but I think this is going to be a very, *very* good night.

[4]

MARISSA

WE MAKE out in the backseat of the car.

We make out as we're waiting for the elevator.

We make out in the elevator.

Finally, we step into Vince's place on the top floor, and he immediately shoves me against the door, unzips the side of my dress, and fills his hands with my breasts. When he leans back, he graces me with a devilish smile.

Damn, he's handsome.

Danger! screams my brain.

I date safe guys. Good guys. Ones who treat me well. I've never broken up with a guy because he was a piece of shit.

But I'm not dating Vince, I remind my overactive brain. And even if he's a playboy, he's been good to me. Checking that I was onboard with what he was doing. Making sure I didn't have too much to drink. And he was willing to leave the party, to somewhere I felt more comfortable.

Yes, this is just what I need.

He bends down to kiss me again. He's at least six inches taller than me, but I'm pretty short, so I'm sure he's no more than five-ten. Not so tall that he's impossible to kiss while standing up. Perfect.

He dips his head farther and wraps his lips around one of my breasts. Taking as much into his mouth as he can, swirling his tongue over my nipple. I arch against him, and then I untuck his shirt and slide my hands up his warm skin. Vince is lean, not hugely muscled, but there are certainly some hard muscles going on here. I scrape my fingernails over him, and my nipple pops out of his mouth as he groans.

The way he responds to me—it gives me such a high.

I unbuckle his belt and slide my hand into his boxer briefs. His cock is hard and rigid. It makes my inner muscles clench, and I'm very aware that I'm not wearing panties.

"Marissa."

I love that he's saying my name. I don't feel like I'm interchangeable with all the women who have come before me—and I know there have been an awful lot of women.

But he makes me feel like I'm the only one who matters.

Danger! Danger!

No, I'll be fine. I know exactly what I'm getting myself into, and I know what this isn't.

He pushes up my dress until it's a thick belt around my waist and slides two fingers inside me. It's a damn good thing I'm against the door, because my knees feel weak.

His lips curve in another of his devastating smiles, and then he's kissing me again as he finger-fucks me and I jack him off.

It's not enough.

I want.

Want, want, want.

I can't have everything I desire in life, but for tonight, I can take this.

"Please," I say desperately.

He slides his hands under my ass and lifts me up. I'm so close to being impaled on his cock...

"Condom." Through the haze of lust, I still remember to use protection.

"I was just getting to that."

He sets me down and pulls a condom out of his pocket. My red underwear falls out at the same time, but he leaves it on the floor. Once he's sheathed himself, he lifts me up again. I breathe shallowly.

I want. I want. I want.

He brings me down on his cock, and I cry out as he fills me.

He feels amazing.

I wrap my legs around him and hold on tight. My bare back rubs against the door as he thrusts in and out, and it's not exactly comfortable, though somehow it heightens the pleasure.

"Oh, fuck," I murmur.

He grins, but then he shoves deep inside me, and that grin is wiped away and he looks...overcome.

That was me. I did that to him.

He kisses me as he shoves inside me over and over. The pleasure is so sharp and intense, I'm barely able to kiss him back, but I do my best as I cling to him, loving the slide of his lips over mine.

When he slips one hand between us and touches my clit, however, I lose the ability to do anything other than moan.

I spiral up and up. Yes, so close, just one more...

He pumps into me and circles my clit, and I scream.

He quickens his pace, finishing inside me a moment later. When he pulls out and sets me on my feet, I slump against the door.

"You good?" he asks, placing his finger under my chin and tipping it up.

"Yeah." I laugh. "Yeah, I'm good."

He kisses me again, but this kiss is different from all the others. It's missing the sharp desperation, though it's still a kiss of desire.

"Oh my God." I pull away. "I didn't even take off my boots! I'm sorry. I'm a terrible guest." I get to work on unlacing them.

"If you'd tried, I wouldn't have let you. And you're a lovely guest, don't worry."

We take off our footwear, and then he carries me through the penthouse, into the bedroom. He sets me on the bed and flicks on the lights, then disposes of the dress that's bunched around my waist. I remove his jacket and unbutton his shirt, revealing the fine chest that I've only touched before, not seen.

His pants and boxer briefs are next, and now we're naked together.

We had sex first, and then we took off our clothes.

I can't help chuckling.

"Why me?" he asks.

"What do you mean?"

"You walked over to me right after you saw me kissing another woman. Was it my reputation? You wanted to know what it would be like with Vince Fong?" He doesn't sound bothered by this.

"I thought you were handsome—even though I could only see the side of your face—and there was something about the way you were touching her… I wanted you to touch me the same way. I didn't know who you were until Carrie told me, though."

All that matters is that tonight, he's with me. If anything, his extensive sexual history kind of turns me on.

I take his hand and press it to my bare shoulder. Even though I orgasmed not ten minutes ago, his touch sizzles.

I still want.

And I can't help being impressed that he's already getting hard again.

His lips quirk up when he sees me looking at the erection bobbing between his legs, and then he slides down my body and sets his mouth to my clit.

"Yes," I say, keeping his head in place with my hand.

"You're insatiable."

"Before tonight, I hadn't had sex in almost a year."

He looks utterly horrified.

"So I'm looking for a *lot* of sex tonight." Even I'm surprised by how insatiable I am. Yes, I've had a dry streak, but I feel like I could have sex all night long, like I'm twenty-one again.

"Then you've come to the right man."

It's well after midnight, and I haven't been awake this late in a long time, responsible thirty-six-year-old that I am.

"You want a drink?" Vince asks. "I've got wine, beer, bourbon, whiskey…"

"Nah, I'm good."

I'm very good, indeed. We've had several rounds of sex, and I'm finally sated.

"I also have some special gummies," he says.

"No, there's nothing I need."

My stomach, naturally, thinks this is a great opportunity to growl in protest. Not the sort of noise that pairs well with a hot one-night stand.

"Sorry," I say, embarrassed.

"I can get you some food. There's leftover pizza."

And that's how Vince and I end up feeding each other cold pizza with pepperoni, mushrooms, and green pepper.

I thought I was done with sex for the night, but pizza gives me the energy for one more round.

I stretch my arms above my head and look at the clock.

It's nine thirty in the morning. I just had a solid eight hours of sleep after the best sex of my life. I wiggle this way and that. I'm a little sore, but it's delightful. I enjoy feeling like my body's been used.

Last night was just what I needed, after all the stress I've had lately.

"Hey," Vince says, sitting up. "You sleep well?"

"Yeah."

He looks as gorgeous in the morning light as he did last night at the party, but his hair is mussed now and he's not wearing a shirt. Actually, we're both still naked, and I'm not complaining.

I press myself against his side and glide my fingers over his pecs.

"I know exactly what I want for breakfast," I murmur.

"Cold pizza again?" he asks with a smile. "Or cereal and milk?"

"Mmm." I slide down his body and wrap my hand around his hardening cock. "If you're interested, that is."

"Oh, I'm definitely interested."

I lick up the underside of his cock, nice and slow.

When I was younger, I never could have been this bold with a man I'd known for all of twelve hours. I never could have pulled off a line like, *I know exactly what I want for breakfast.* In fact, I never could have slept with Vince in the first place.

But as I've gotten older, I've become less self-conscious, better at grabbing what I want from life.

As I take him in my mouth, need builds up inside me.

I grab a condom from the bedside table and roll it on, and then I sink down on his cock and release an unsteady breath.

Sex is different in the morning. There are no shadows to hide anything. Our pace is more languid. I ride him with deep, sensual strokes, palming my breasts; he can't take his eyes off me.

I adjust my angle to get some friction from my clit rubbing against him.

Yes, that's good.

My orgasm takes me by surprise. One moment I'm starting to

get close, and the next, I'm over the edge, practically sobbing in pleasure, and Vince flips us over.

It takes me a minute to recover, and then, to my frustration, he stops moving.

"What's your favorite movie?" he asks, grinning down at me.

"You bastard." I try to roll us back over so I'm on top, but he's too strong.

"I haven't heard of that one. Is it recent?"

I'm not sure I've rolled my eyes when having sex before, but there's a first time for everything.

"Come on, Vince."

"Is that a movie about me? I suppose the title is appropriate."

I shoot him a withering look.

"Okay, okay."

He licks my nipple just the way I like it—he's a quick study—before he begins thrusting again. God, he fills me just perfectly.

"I like you better when you're doing, not talking," I say, and he laughs.

We move in tandem until we tumble over the edge at the same time. Even though we haven't known each other for long, it's as though we're already in sync.

When we collapse on our backs afterward, he says, "You have anything to do today?"

I shake my head.

"How about we make this a two-night stand instead?" He speaks with the confidence of a man who knows he won't be turned down.

I want to wipe that smug smile off his face.

But even more than that, I want to spend more time with him.

I open my mouth to answer, but then his phone rings.

"Sorry, I have to get that." He takes the call. "Hi, Po Po."

His grandma. It's rather charming that he's interrupted our conversation for her.

"Yes," he says. "I'll be there." He gets up and starts casually walking around the room—in the nude—as he speaks to his grandmother. It seems wrong, but I won't deny I'm enjoying the view. "That happened one time... One time! I promise, I won't forget."

A part of me finds it disorienting that he's talking to his grandma in English. In fact, part of me is disoriented by the fact that Vince Fong has a family, period, even though I know a little about them. He's just not the kind of guy you imagine talking to his mom or grandma.

"No, you didn't wake me up," he continues, "but I can't talk for long... Yes... I know. *I know*... Okay. Bye."

When he ends the call, I see the background picture on his screen before he turns it off. Perhaps there's a lot I don't know about Vince.

Not surprising. After all, I have only one night, plus his reputation, to go on.

"Do you have a baby?" I ask.

"Nah, that's my niece. Evie." He smiles as he turns the screen back on and shows me a picture of him and Evie together. "That was yesterday afternoon."

"She's a cutie," I say. Evie has pudgy cheeks and an adorable tooth-free smile. "How's her mother doing?"

Babies are cute, but whenever I see one, I'm concerned about the mother. Pregnancy and caring for a baby can be difficult. My friend Pearl had it pretty rough.

But I don't even know who Evie's mother is. I shouldn't have asked.

"She's well," Vince says, then flips to a picture of Evie and Pusheen.

And, okay, maybe the sight of the baby with Pusheen causes a slight stab in my chest. I always thought I'd be a mother, even though I know motherhood can be tough. I imagined I'd get married and have a baby and a house, and my child would grow up with a dad.

Unlike me.

My dad was, by all accounts, a fun and loving man, a devoted father.

But he died when I was three.

And now my biological clock is ticking, and I still can't find the right guy.

"You okay?" Vince touches my shoulder.

"I'm fine."

He sits behind me and wraps his arms around my chest. I think he wants to ask why I look a bit sad, but he can tell I'd prefer not to talk about it.

Vince Fong is kinder and more thoughtful than I expected.

"So, how do you feel about a two-night stand?" he asks. "I have nothing planned until tomorrow evening, when I'm having dinner with my family. What do you say we spend all that time together?"

I'm having dinner with Mom and Larry tomorrow, but that's it.

And there are a few things I'd like to forget about now. More sex is just what I need.

More sex with *Vince*, specifically.

"Yes," I say.

"Perfect." He turns me around to face him. "I'd like you to spend most of this weekend without any clothes on. Sound like a plan?"

"It sure does."

$$[\ 5\ ]$$

VINCE

MARISSA IS STANDING at my door, in the black dress and black boots she was wearing when I met her almost forty-eight hours ago.

And what a great forty-eight hours it's been.

True to my word, she spent most of those hours naked. When she was wearing clothes, it was simply one of my T-shirts, and I'm not gonna lie, it was hot seeing her in my clothes.

"So..." She seems a little shy now. "Thanks for the great weekend."

"It was my pleasure," I say.

"You certainly seemed to experience a lot of pleasure." She's smirking.

I feel like she's stolen my line.

I rack my brain for something else to say. I'm usually pretty good at opening my mouth and having words spew out, but right now, I'm struggling.

This was the best weekend I've had in a long, long time. I'd been a little bored with my life of lazy luxury. The parties, the women...I don't do it as much as I used to, and it seemed a bit routine, like I did it because I didn't know what else to do with myself.

But the weekend with Marissa?

This was different.

I felt *alive*.

Yesterday evening, we ordered Vietnamese food—we didn't go outside all weekend, ordering in whenever we got hungry—and as I looked at her over my steaming bowl of pho, I had the fleeting thought that life couldn't get any better than this.

Curious, that.

Afterward, we had some of my special cherry gummies, and getting high with Marissa was pretty great, too.

A part of me wants to ask to see her again, but I told her that I only wanted two nights, nothing more. In fact, I don't even know what more would look like. I haven't had a girlfriend since university, over a decade ago.

"Hope you enjoy your dinner with your family," I say.

"You, too."

And then she's gone, all five foot two of her.

I'm always clear about what I can offer, but sometimes women get ideas and think they'll be the one to change me, and they hang around. Marissa didn't do that. Stupidly, I kind of wished she had.

But this is for the best.

"What were you doing when I called yesterday?" Po Po asks.

I'm sitting at the dining room table in my childhood home. My parents, my grandmother, my brothers, and my sister-in-law are here. Baby Evie is sleeping.

I shrug. If it was just me and my brothers, I'd tell the truth. *I was naked in bed with a woman.* Julian would roll his eyes in exasperation, and I always enjoy making him do that. Or maybe I'd play it up a little and say I was in the middle of an orgy.

But I wouldn't say in front of my grandma, who is ninety-one years old and already thinks I'm enough of a shit disturber.

"Just reading in bed," I say.

Julian snorts.

"Lying is a sin," Cedric says.

"Who, me? Lie?" I say, as though I've never heard a more insulting thing in my life. "Yeah, you're right. I would never do something as mundane as reading a book."

Cedric is a writer. Or *was* a writer, as he keeps saying now, since he hasn't written in a few years. His first book was pretty successful, but he has yet to produce a follow-up. He teaches at one of the colleges in the city now.

The truth is, I do read a little, but I keep pretending I don't so that I can say I never read Cedric's book.

I did, in fact, read it.

I did not, alas, like it.

It was boring and had too much navel-gazing for my liking.

"What were you actually doing?" Po Po asks, putting down her chopsticks. "Aiyah, I never know when you are telling the truth and when you are lying."

"In all honesty"—a lie, of course—"I hadn't been up for long and was just making some coffee before playing videogames. Solid Saturday morning."

"Maybe we should start surprising you with visits," Mom says, "and see what you're really doing."

She sure knows how to strike fear into the heart of a man.

"Not a good idea," Cedric says. "You never know what you could find."

"Exactly," Mom says. "That's why I want to do it."

"You might wish you hadn't," Julian murmurs.

The truth is, most of the time when I'm home, I'm not doing anything too exciting. Videogames are a frequent pastime, yes.

Binge-watching shows on Netflix. Keeping tabs on my investments.

The more exciting stuff usually happens away from home, though I do host parties on occasion, and sometimes I have guests like Marissa.

The thought of my family interrupting such encounters is downright terrifying. My dad did that once, and I'm still recovering.

Fortunately, I think this is an empty threat.

My mother doesn't make any more threats during the rest of dinner and dessert. Courtney feeds Evie, and then I hold my niece for a while.

When I get home, I play videogames before going to bed at midnight.

I can't sleep, though. I stare at my ceiling and sigh.

How did I get here? What is the point of my life?

Nothing good ever comes from thinking about these questions.

I built a company and sold it for tons of money. I was good at it. I was *great* at it. But the thought of going back to that world scares the crap out of me. There have been offers from friends to join in their new ventures, and I always listen, then say it's not quite right for me.

I remember the exhaustion and insomnia. The irritability, the cynicism—which isn't like me at all. I remember the way I couldn't focus and was barely functional by the end. Years later, I'm still picking up the pieces.

It destroyed my mental health, something that Courtney has helped me acknowledge.

When my family showed up at Julian's office and demanded he take two weeks off work, my mother said she was worried about his health and feared he'd burn out, but I didn't admit that I was worried, too. I mean, it's Julian, and he's always been good with hard work and pressure, but still. I couldn't help thinking of my own experience.

Though I feel rather aimless now, it's better to be a useless playboy than do something like that again.

I push these thoughts aside and roll over. Marissa isn't there next to me, like she was the last two nights. She didn't snore or hog the blankets, but she sprawled out while she was sleeping and nearly hit me in the face at one point.

I miss her.

Well, that's just because of all the great sex, because she gave me the best weekend I'd had in a long time. Next weekend should be good, too. Brian and I are visiting a friend in NYC, and we always have fun there.

I fall asleep thinking of Marissa.

[6]

MARISSA

"How was your weekend?" Mom asks, lifting her chopsticks to her lips.

"It was good," I say brightly. "Saw some friends and went shopping. Did some chores."

I give her a big smile, not as an attempt to sell my lie, but because I'm thrilled she's okay. I'd worried so much about the tumor, even though she kept telling me not to worry.

But I can't lose my mother.

I had no other family in Canada when I was growing up. Every four years, we'd go to Hong Kong, and those trips were always awkward. My maternal grandmother would spend much of the time begging my mother to move back. I had a few cousins, but they were a lot older than me. My father's family was furious with my mother, even a decade after his death, which they thought was her fault. To them, Canada killed him; if he and my mom had never moved, he would still be alive. They also blamed her for not giving my father a son.

Without my mother, I would feel like I had no family.

Though there's Larry, of course. My mother's husband. She never dated when I was a child, but she met him once I got a job and moved out. He's white. He was widowed in his forties, and his kids are a few years younger than me.

So, I've got Larry and my "step siblings," but that's different. I didn't meet them until I'd been an adult for almost a decade.

After they got married five years ago, Larry sold his house, and he and Mom bought a little townhome in Scarborough. He's not rich, but he and my mom are able to afford a decent retirement with trips a couple times a year, so I'm happy with how it worked out.

Mom deserves it, after everything.

Tonight, it's just me; Larry's kids, who live out of town, aren't here. Larry has made beef stroganoff, something I'd never eaten before I met him, but for some reason, Larry *loves* beef stroganoff, and he makes it all the time. I'm just glad Mom doesn't have to do all the cooking.

"What projects do you have at work?" Mom asks.

"Do you really want to hear about this?" I don't mind my job, but it's not super exciting to talk about with people outside the field.

"Yes, you sound so smart!" She smiles at me.

My mother didn't push me hard and have ridiculous expectations like many of my friends' parents did. She was too busy struggling to make ends meet, and I think she understood that I already felt a lot of pressure without her saying anything. She's never bugged me about getting married and having children, either. Occasionally she asks if I'm seeing anyone, but that's about it.

Though I don't keep a lot of secrets from my mom, of course I don't tell her about the guy I had sex with a dozen times in forty-eight hours. (Okay, maybe it was only nine times, but still.) And I don't tell her about those cherry gummies.

When I get back to my condo near Eglinton and Mount Pleasant, I receive a text from Carrie.

How was your night? she asks. *Is Vince as good in bed as the rumors say?*

I grin as I type. *Oh, yeah. Vince was great.*

Details.

Nope. Those are just for me.

But you slept with Vince Fong! And you're such a badass that you walked right up to him and started making out with him.

Yeah, and he gave me an orgasm in public.

I'm not really an exhibitionist, but for some reason, it was just what I needed on Friday.

Wow. That was only two days ago. It feels like so much longer.

I am pretty badass, aren't I? I text. *How was your night?*

I went home with Alexis, actually.

Well, I'm glad the woman I saw kissing Vince still got to have a good time.

That night, when I cuddle up under my covers, I'm at peace with the world, though I experience a moment of longing to feel Vince's hand drifting down my body again. Then I remind myself that he's not the kind of guy I want long-term.

It was just one glorious weekend, and that's okay.

The next few weeks proceed as usual. I go to work. I come home and make myself dinner and eat alone. I read, I watch TV. I sign up for a new dating app and immediately get a message from a creepy dude. I talk to my mother on the phone.

I listen to an Everclear album and remember when Vince asked about my favorite song.

While he had his fingers inside me.

Yeah, that was me.

I rarely have such experiences, but now I've got some very hot memories to pull up when I use my vibrator.

Life proceeds more or less as usual…until it doesn't.

My cycles have always been fairly regular. I can predict when I'll get my period, plus or minus a day.

When I'm two days late, I start to worry.

When I'm three days late, I buy a pregnancy test.

I pee on the stick first thing the next morning and wait two minutes, like it says.

I've taken pregnancy tests before. The first time, I wasn't pregnant. I got my period the next day; I was probably late because I was worried about my exams.

The second time, I was pregnant.

The third time, I wasn't pregnant.

And this time…

Oh dear God, I'm pregnant.

[7]

MARISSA

I'M pregnant and Vince Fong is the father.

I let out a burst of unhinged laughter.

No, this can't be happening. We used condoms every time. We had no problems with them breaking or slipping off. Yes, there was a bit of booze and pot that weekend, but I had my wits about me the whole time.

Does he have some kind of super sperm?

Last time, it wasn't like this at all. I had a serious boyfriend, and we'd stopped using condoms because I was on the pill. But then I got sick and had to take antibiotics, which apparently can affect the efficacy of the pill.

Nobody told me, and I got pregnant.

I never considered keeping it. I'd just started my last year of undergrad and was not in a place to have a baby. Sanjay was supportive of my decision.

I don't regret that abortion, not one bit. If I hadn't terminated the pregnancy, I'd have a teenager now.

Denial won't get me anywhere; I have to accept it. The chance of a false positive is very low.

I am pregnant.

And I'm not with the father.

As a woman who grew up with a single parent, the one thing I desperately want for my kid is two loving parents, as well as some level of financial security.

I can't keep this pregnancy. I'll have an abortion like last time. No big deal.

Except it doesn't sit right with me.

I drop to the edge of the bathtub, head in my hands.

What if this is my last chance? I'm not getting any younger.

I swore I'd never go the sperm-donor route because I didn't want to be a single mom, even though I think I'd be a good mother.

I would have given anything to spend a little time with my own father. I always dreamed my child would have that connection, the one I didn't have.

But although Vince and I aren't together, that doesn't mean he can't be part of the child's life. I doubt he'd want to be heavily involved—it would cramp his wild bachelor lifestyle—but he's a decent guy.

He's definitely not the worst father I could imagine for my child.

And he had a picture of his little niece on his phone and seemed rather taken with her. It's not much to go on, but he loves that child, and he would love ours, wouldn't he? He'd be the cool father who'd show up a few times a month and spoil the kid rotten. I'd have to be the disciplinarian, but that's okay.

I can't believe I'm having a baby with a man I hardly know.

Because yes, I think I'm going to have this baby.

The child will have their cool father, and maybe I'll be able to give them a stepfather, too.

The child will also have their grandmother, and they can call Larry "grandpa." Grandparents, right here in the city! Larry's daughter and her wife have a kid. A cousin!

Then I think of Vince's family, and it's nearly enough to make me sob. He has a grandmother who calls him on Saturday morning. He has parents and brothers and a niece. All in Toronto, I think.

My child could be spending holidays with the Fongs. They're giants in the Chinese community here. Being part of that family would be a huge advantage.

And then there's the money.

It seems wrong to think of it now, but I can't help it.

Vince is rich, and his family is rich. I have zero idea how child support works, but surely he could provide one or two thousand a month or pay for childcare. He'd hardly feel that.

I make decent money and have a comfortable life. I could afford a child, although it would be a bit tough, seeing as Toronto is far from a cheap city. But with a little help from Vince, it would be no problem.

I take a few deep breaths. I'm starting to feel better. I've thought about it logically, haven't I? Sure, this isn't what I imagined, but I can make it work.

Who would have thought that a hot two-night stand would lead to *this*? My one wild weekend of stress relief?

Yeah, this child is never, ever going to hear the story of how I met their father. I'll just say something vague like, "We met through friends."

It's not even a lie.

After work today, I'll get some prenatal vitamins and schedule a doctor's appointment. And then I'll contact Vince. I don't want to tell anyone else until I've talked to him. There's a small chance he won't want to be involved.

If so, what will I do?

Telling your fling that you're pregnant seems like something that should be done in private, so I've invited Vince to my condo.

Fortunately, I already had his phone number. I asked for it before he took me home from the party, then texted it to Carrie, just in case.

Yesterday, I told him that I wanted to see him again, no more details.

He agreed.

And now I'm sitting at my kitchen table, waiting.

My phone rings. I buzz him up, then start pacing. What if Vince isn't who I think he is? I only spent one weekend with him. I'm basing some of my assumptions on the two seconds I saw him looking at the picture of his niece.

Oh, no.

I feel queasy.

Is it nerves? Or morning sickness?

I know morning sickness isn't necessarily limited to the mornings. Pearl puked all day long. For three months. God, could I handle puking all day for three months?

There's a knock on the door. My heart pounding, I open it up.

As soon as I see Vince, wearing a winter jacket on top of jeans and a sweater, I decide to just get it over with. I was going to make tea, and I'd bought some cookies, hoping that would somehow make the news go down easier.

But fuck it.

"I'm pregnant and you're the father and I'm keeping it," I say in a rush.

He looks at me like he didn't understand a word I said.

"I'm pregnant," I repeat.

He says nothing, just nods.

"And you're definitely the father. I haven't been with anyone else in a long time."

He nods again.

"And I'm planning to keep it."

Vince just looks at me for another moment. My heartbeat

quickens, and I worry he's pissed and won't want anything to do with this child.

"I'm going to be a dad?" he says, and it sounds…hopeful.

"Assuming everything goes well, yeah."

He grins.

I did not expect this reaction, but as the seconds tick by, his grin only grows.

"It's important to me that you're involved," I say.

"Of course."

Vince envelops me in a hug

And then he does something I *really* did not expect.

He drops to one knee, takes my hand, and says, "Will you marry me?"

[8]

VINCE

MARISSA RESPONDS to my proposal by kicking me in the shin.

"Stop messing with me," she says.

"I'm not messing with you," I insist. "Let's get married."

When Marissa asked me to come over, I figured she wanted to have sex again. Usually, I would have said no, but she's been haunting my dreams and I crave her touch.

But that's not what happened.

A baby like Evie. But *mine*.

As soon as I wrapped my head around the idea, I loved it.

Now I have a purpose in life, the thing that eluded me for so long.

The picture in my mind is crystal clear. Me, Marissa, and a cute little bundle that giggles when I press their nose. The three of us.

It's not often I set my mind to anything, but once I do, I get it done.

I'm going to make that image a reality.

Yes, it's impulsive. That's who I am. I walked in here five minutes ago with zero intention of proposing. In fact, I'd never seriously thought of marriage before in my life. My university girlfriend and I may have talked about it vaguely. Later, I had no time for a relationship, and after I sold the company, I just wanted to have fun. I didn't want commitment.

When Julian started seeing Courtney, I did think about relationships briefly but figured it just wasn't me. Secretly, I also wondered if I was unlovable and too broken for a relationship.

But now, I know what I need in my life. This will make me whole.

"You can't propose to me just because we're having a baby," Marissa says.

"Why not?"

"A baby outside of marriage isn't some big scandal now. I appreciate your attempt to do the right thing, something I don't think you're well acquainted with—"

I interrupt her words with a peal of laughter.

Yeah, I like this woman.

"Darling," I drawl. "You—"

"I haven't agreed to marry you. Don't calling me 'darling.'"

"Fine. Marissa, you are correct. But I want this, I do. You, me, and the baby. I think we can make it work. Why not?"

"I'm not marrying someone I barely know. It's ridiculous. If we were together, maybe it would be different, but I can't even imagine you having a girlfriend, let alone getting married. I'm sure you'll feel differently tomorrow."

I finally get up from the floor and sit on a chair. "I'll feel the same way, and for your information, I've had relationships before." I'm pleased I can prove her wrong.

"How long was the longest one? Three weeks?"

"Try two years."

She seems vaguely impressed. Then she narrows her eyes. "When was this?"

"Let me think...I believe we broke up when I was twenty-two."

"Exactly."

"Well, neither of us has had a kid before." I pause. "You don't have a kid, do you?"

"I do not."

"But we'll figure that out. We can figure out marriage, too."

"Vince." She grits her teeth. "I'm not marrying a man I don't love."

"I'm very lovable." I bat my eyelashes.

She snorts out a reluctant laugh.

The truth, however, is that my words are all false bravado.

I know I'm likable. Entertaining. The kind of guy people enjoy having around. But lovable? I'm still not sure about that. I fear I'm all flash and no substance, a bit of a mess. If someone really gets to know me, will they want what they see?

"And you don't love me," she says. "We've spent all of one weekend together."

"Some people fall in love at first sight."

"You fell in love when I walked up to you and shoved my tongue down your throat?"

I pretend to think about this as I look Marissa up and down. Today, she's wearing jeans and a pink sweater—nothing as glamorous as the night I met her, but she's a beautiful woman, even if she seems a little annoyed with me.

"That's lust," she says.

"I know. I don't love you," I admit, "but I think I'll come to love you. I mean, we have great chemistry, and that weekend we spent together was the best time I'd had in months." I used to be pretty doubtful about my ability to love, but that's changed in recent months, even if I have doubts that someone could feel that way about *me*.

Her face softens. "It was pretty great. And now we have to deal with the consequences."

"We used a condom every time, didn't we?" I ask, but I'm pretty sure of the answer. I'm always careful about condoms.

"Yeah. Have you ever gotten anyone pregnant before?"

"Not that I know of." This birth control failure is a first for me.

She looks down. "I got pregnant in undergrad. I terminated it right away. There was no way I was prepared to be a parent."

I still. "Are you thinking of terminating this one? You said you're keeping it."

It's her choice, of course, but I've already become attached to the idea.

"I wasn't completely sure I would if you weren't onboard, but I'm definitely keeping it now. I've always wanted a child, and I'm at a good place in my life."

"But you're not in a good place to get married."

"To someone I don't love? Hell no. That's not an option for me, ever." She pauses. "I figure I'll have custody, and you can visit once or twice a week. When the child gets a little older, you can have one weeknight and one or two weekends a month."

"I want to be more involved."

"Sure. And you'll tell your family? You won't keep this a secret from them?"

"Of course not."

"I didn't have any extended family in Canada. I want that for my child."

"Absolutely."

She smiles faintly. "I thought you'd want to be a little involved, but not a lot. I figured it wouldn't fit with your lifestyle."

"I'm not attached to my lifestyle."

She shakes her head, not believing me, I expect. "I'm glad you want to be an important part of the child's life, but I still don't think you actually want to get married—not that I'd say yes anyway. You're just overwhelmed by the news and don't know what to make of it. Besides, you're not the kind of guy I'd even date."

I'm not surprised, but it still stings a little. "Why not?"

"Because you're…you. You've always got a different woman in your bed. You're known for partying all night and jetting off to glamorous locations and doing who knows what kind of drugs."

"That part is mostly exaggeration." There was a point when I tried a lot of things, but now, I'm pretty tame.

Which is probably still wild from Marissa's point of view. The night at Brian's was an anomaly for her, whereas it was just business as usual for me.

But I'm kind of tired of that life, and I've been wanting something to do with myself.

This? It's perfect.

I just have to convince her.

I'll prove that I can be everything she thinks I'm not. I can't blame her for the view she has of me. I've cultivated that persona.

But it's not all I am.

"I'll come to your appointments," I say. "Have you had any yet?"

"I'm seeing my doctor next week, but there's no need for you to come to that."

"I want to."

She sighs. "I don't feel comfortable discussing my health in front of you."

"Let me drive you there and back, then. Sit in the waiting room."

"Okay."

I refrain from pumping my fist in victory.

She won't marry me, but she'll let me drive her to an appointment! It's a start.

"Of course, there's a chance I might miscarry," she says. "I haven't told anyone else about the pregnancy yet, but I plan to tell my mother and a friend. I'd like you to wait until I've gotten to twelve weeks before telling your family, though."

"No problem."

I leave Marissa's place several minutes later, after she insists on feeding me cookies. She awkwardly gives me a hug and says she'll text me the details of the appointment.

I smile as I wait for the elevator. I'm going to be a dad and a husband! Sure, she rejected my proposal, but somehow, I'm going to do it. Marissa…

Oh, shit, I don't even know her last name.

Well, I will learn Marissa's last name, and then I'll hopefully get her to fall in love with me and accept my marriage proposal.

There's a slight twinge in my chest at the thought.

I have some serious doubts that this is all possible—will she really be able to love me?—but I'm trying to be optimistic.

I hope that optimism isn't misplaced.

[9]

MARISSA

Maybe this was a mistake.

I'm standing in the parking lot at work, bundled up in my winter jacket. It's freaking cold. I've only been outside for a minute, and my teeth are already chattering.

I look at my watch again. Vince is supposed to pick me up in three minutes.

When he offered to drive me, I thought I'd give him a chance to prove he's a little responsible. Besides, my doctor's office is near Yonge and Eglinton, and the traffic and parking situation is a nightmare around there, thanks to the LRT construction. It would be nice to let someone else deal with that.

But now I'm convinced he's going to be late.

I pull my toque lower over my ears and look at my watch again. It's eleven thirty-eight, and I'm supposed to be taking a long lunch to have this doctor's appointment. If he's not here in five minutes, I'm driving myself.

Just then, a black sports car screeches into the parking lot and pulls up in front of me. Vince jumps out of the driver's seat and runs around to open the passenger's door.

"That's really not necessary," I tell him.

In response, he smiles.

He really is a handsome man. Maybe he'll pass those good looks onto our baby. I still can't believe I'm having a baby with this guy.

He gets in the car, and we're off.

"You thought I wasn't going to show up on time, didn't you?" he says.

"I, uh…"

"You have so little faith in me. It hurts." He doesn't sound hurt at all, though. He presses his hand to his heart before putting it back on the steering wheel. "It's okay, I don't blame you." He graces me with another winning smile. "By the way, what's your last name? I realized I'd proposed to a woman without even knowing her last name."

"It's Chan."

"Marissa Chan, you might be skeptical, but my proposal was serious. I've had a week to think about it, and I'm not retracting it. The proposal is still on the table, if you ever change your mind. Which I hope you will."

I do not understand this man. At all. He's a legendary playboy, and yet when I told him I was having his baby, he wanted to marry me?

"As I told you," I say, "I'm not marrying a man I don't love. Nor am I marrying a man I don't believe could be faithful to me."

He whips his head toward me before turning back to the road. "I can be faithful." This time, he does sound a bit hurt. "Actually, I haven't been with anyone since you, and I promise to be faithful to you from now on."

"We're not in a relationship, Vince."

"I'll do it anyway, just to prove it to you."

"I'll have no way of knowing if you're telling the truth."

"I guess you'll just have to trust me."

I don't know what to say. Should I trust him? Yes, he has his reputation, but he's been pretty good to me. He was an attentive lover, and he picked me up exactly when he said he would. I shouldn't assume his history of casual sex means he couldn't be faithful if he wanted.

"I'll try," I say.

"Good. How have you been feeling?"

"Not too bad." I don't feel like telling him about the fatigue and swollen breasts.

We sit in silence for the rest of the drive. Vince drops me off right out front, then goes to park the car and returns five minutes later.

When he sits down, he opens up an enormous book on pregnancy. He's two-thirds of the way through the book.

I feel like a slouch.

And *I'm* the one who's pregnant.

I'm touched, although perhaps he's doing this all for show.

"Look at this." He pulls out his phone and opens an app. "It tells you what to expect for each week of pregnancy and how big the fetus is and…lots of other things."

Oh. It never even occurred to me to look for a pregnancy app.

"Can you text me the name of it?" I ask.

"Sure thing." A moment later, my phone pings. "I was wondering…do you plan on finding out the sex of the baby? I mean, not now, obviously. It's too early."

"I'm not sure."

"Do you have a preference? Boy or girl?"

"No, but it's easier to imagine having a girl. It was just my mom and me growing up, so that's what pops into my head."

Me and my little girl against the world.

But with Vince. And an extended family. And no money worries.

"I imagine us having a girl, too," Vince says. "Because my niece is the only baby I know. But I'm fine either way."

"The one thing we are not having is a gender reveal party. I know showy stuff is your thing—"

"You seem to have a lot of preconceived notions about me," he murmurs, "but I agree. No gender reveal party."

"What about a cake smashing party for our baby's first birthday?"

"A cake smashing party?"

"You buy a pretty cake and take lots of photos as your child destroys it. Apparently adult cake smashing parties are a thing, too, if you're interested in doing that yourself and making a mess with buttercream."

We look at each other and laugh. We're still laughing when the doctor comes out to get me for the appointment, and for a moment, it feels like we're a real couple.

When I walk out of the doctor's office, Vince next to me, I'm feeling good.

"She did a blood test to confirm the pregnancy," I say, "and she ordered my twelve-week ultrasound plus other tests and referred me to an ob-gyn. We also talked a bit about pregnancy in my old age. Since, you know, it's a geriatric pregnancy."

"Say what?"

"I'm over thirty-five."

"I didn't realize that."

"How old did you think I was?"

He shrugs. "My age. I'm thirty-three."

"Well, I'm thirty-six. You can add that to the list of things you know about me. I'll be thirty-seven by the time the baby comes."

"Hardly *geriatric*. You want to grab a quick lunch before I drive you back?"

"Yeah, that would be good."

"There's a Chinese place nearby. I was looking at the reviews on Yelp."

I shake my head. "I went there once. The servers are too friendly. Made me suspicious. And sure enough, it wasn't that great."

He laughs. "I know what you mean. What do you want?"

"The falafel shop near here is pretty good." I look at my watch. "I should be getting back to the office."

"You have to eat first. Or did you bring a lunch?"

"I didn't."

"Falafels to go, then."

I lead him to the falafel and shawarma place. I get a falafel sandwich with everything on it, including lots of pickles—for some reason I'm in a pickle mood today. I really am quite hungry, so I start eating my sandwich right away, but I put it aside once we get into Vince's car.

"You can eat in the car, I don't mind," he says as he pulls away from the curb.

"Umm." I don't know much about cars, but I can tell this is a fancy one. And it's spotless.

My stomach growls.

"Eat the damn falafels, Marissa Chan. My car will survive. It's important to eat properly during pregnancy."

I roll my eyes. "I can take care of myself."

"I know. But let me worry about taking care of the car."

"Fine. Be that way."

"I know, I'm so difficult, wanting to make sure you eat enough."

"Bastard," I mutter.

He laughs.

Fifteen minutes later, I've finished my very tasty falafel sandwich and we've arrived at my office.

"Thank you for the ride," I say.

"You're welcome. If you need anything, ever, feel free to text me, alright? You're not doing this alone."

I smile at Vince, then get out of the car.

Though he's not the father I imagined for my child, I think this might work out okay.

But I am *not* going to marry him.

[10]

MARISSA

I ALWAYS DO my grocery shopping on Saturday morning.

When I finished grad school and moved out three months later after getting a full-time job, I loved grocery shopping. For the first time in my life, I felt rich.

Of course, I was far from rich, and I still had a small student loan to pay off. But my income more than covered my basic expenses, and I could afford to buy what I wanted at the supermarket.

I bought a pint of blueberries, out of season. Havarti that wasn't on sale. Halibut rather than cod, even though cod was cheaper. And when I got something from the olive bar, I really felt like I was living the high life.

I bet Vince Fong has no idea what that's like.

Now grocery shopping has become just another weekly chore, part of the drudgery of being an adult.

But it has never been truly terrible…until today.

I've become really sensitive to smells lately, and someone is cooking mushrooms in the goddamn grocery store.

I approach the little table to see what's going on. An Asian woman, who looks somewhat like my mother, is sautéing mushrooms, which are then placed on top of some kind of fancy cracker with cheese. There's a large pile of crackers and cheese for sale next to her.

She hands over a napkin with one of the cracker/cheese/mushroom delights, and I don't want to be rude, so I take it and curse myself for walking up to the table in the first place.

Normally, I like mushrooms. This is the sort of hors d'oeuvre I'd pick up at a party.

Except today, I feel like I'm going to vomit, and now that I'm holding the offending food, the smell is even stronger.

I turn to the side, and the woman thrusts a garbage can in front of me before I throw up.

Yeah, this is great advertising for the food.

"I'm pregnant," I explain.

I haven't told my friends and family that I'm pregnant yet, but now I've told a woman at the grocery store.

A bunch of people glance in our direction, concerned looks on their faces.

"It's not the food!" I say. "The food is lovely, I'm sure."

Alright. Maybe I'll get my groceries delivered.

The next day, I drive to Mom and Larry's for dinner. When I step into their townhome, a burning smell greets my nose, and Larry is pulling the battery out of the smoke detector.

Fortunately, smoke doesn't make me as queasy as sautéed mushrooms.

"He burnt dinner," Mom says. "But do not worry, I have ordered sushi, including spicy tuna. It's still your favorite, yes?"

I must have a panicked look on my face—I assume that's why she frowns.

"Hey, Marissa," Larry says once the smoke detector has stopped beeping. "You want a glass of wine?"

"Umm." What are they going to offer me next? Soft cheese?

My mother's mouth falls open.

"Are you pregnant?" she asks, just as Larry's kids walk into the hallway.

When I continue to stand there, speechless, she pulls me into the front room, separated from the rest of the floor by French doors.

I'd planned to tell my mother today. I thought I'd pull her aside after dinner and explain the situation, and then she could tell Larry, since I wouldn't expect her to keep secrets from her husband. I certainly hadn't planned on everyone finding out like this.

Man, I'm going to miss spicy tuna rolls. And wine. I love wine.

"Yes, I'm pregnant," I tell my mother once we're seated next to each other on the couch.

She takes my hands in hers. "I had no idea you were trying."

Hahaha. As if.

"What is it like to go to a sperm bank? Do they give you profiles of the sperm donors and you get to choose?"

Oh, Mom.

"The baby was conceived the old-fashioned way."

"But you are not seeing anyone."

"*Mom.* You know that's not required."

She blushes. "Do you know who the father is?" A little worry creeps into her voice.

"I do."

"And? He is a good man?"

"I think so."

"But you don't know him well? I mean, other than…carnally."

When I huff out a laugh, she smiles.

"The father is Vince Fong," I say. "You know who he is?"

"He is a party boy, that's what I've heard."

"Yes, that's where I met him. At a party. But he's been good about this, he really has, and he likes kids." I don't want my mother to dislike him, even though we're not together.

She looks away.

Shit.

I never told her when I got pregnant in university. I thought she'd be disappointed in me, and I can't bear to disappoint my mother. She stayed in this country—where she has no family— after my dad died. For me.

And now I'm knocked up by a notorious playboy. This is not what Good Asian Daughters do.

I've never tried to be perfect, but I did want my mother to be proud of me.

"This is not what I imagined," she admits. "I never wanted to tell you what to do—"

"Why not? Many parents have no qualms about that."

"Because your father would have hated it." She shakes her head. "I hoped you would have children, but I know it is not right to demand grandchildren from you. I thought you would get married and have a little family and a good job…I imagined you would have the life that I didn't. Then when you turned thirty-five, still no man, I wondered if maybe you would go to a sperm bank, because that is what some career women do, isn't it?"

"He offered to marry me." I think this might improve her opinion of Vince.

"And you did not accept?"

"I hardly know him."

"I guess you are right. You should not marry without love. But wouldn't it be nice… He is rich, yes? Not that money is every-thing, but when you are poor, you dream of money." She pauses. "You are happy, though?"

"Yes. I always wanted a child, but not with a sperm donor. I wanted my child to have a second parent because…"

I turn to the side and sniffle into my sleeve.

Grief for a person you don't remember is an odd thing. Cruelly, my first memory is my father's funeral. I remember the smell, more than anything. Shoe polish. I remember my mother crying, I remember feeling so confused.

"I understand," Mom says. "I'm sorry I wanted Cheetos."

"It wasn't your fault."

We sit in silence for a moment.

I've heard so much about my father, and I've seen photos of us together, not just the one on my bedside table. I can picture things in my head. Sometimes, they almost feel like memories, but they're not.

I force a smile. "I'm going to be a mother."

It still seems a bit odd to say that, but I'm excited.

"You will be so good at it." Mom pats my hand. "You know I will give you whatever help I can. I will be the best grandmother. I've already had practice!"

I chuckle. "This is true. And the baby will have Vince's family, too. He has a baby niece. They will be only a year apart. Can you imagine? Having a cousin so close in age?"

"Oh, Marissa," Mom says. "I am so sorry about everything."

"Don't be sorry. You're a good mother."

I pull her into my arms and hug her tight. I never want my mother to feel like she wasn't enough, but I do want my child to grow up with some of the things I didn't have.

"Are you feeling okay?" she asks. "Do you have morning sickness?"

"Yes, unfortunately. It just started."

"For the first trimester, it was like all-day sickness for me. I hope you will not have it quite so bad. But then in the second trimester, I was..." She winks at me. "Horny all the time, is that how you say it?"

"Mom!"

My mother never says things like that.

She laughs at my response.

My heart squeezes. I'm so glad she has a comfortable life now, a nice retirement where she gets to go on holidays. A partner to keep her company. No fear behind her laughs.

"I love you." I pull her into my arms. "But don't ever say stuff like that again."

"I love you, too. I am not disappointed, don't worry. Just surprised. You understand?"

I nod.

"Your father would be proud of you. He would brag about his daughter the engineer. He would be very excited about being a grandpa, I know."

When I was little, I begged my mother for stories about my father all the time, after she'd come home from working long hours at the dry cleaners to make ends meet. He was a hero I could not meet, but he was my dad.

I'm giving my baby something better. A real father.

I brush the back of my hand over my eyes to stem the tears. I'm blaming it on pregnancy hormones. Plus, my mother and I rarely talk about this stuff anymore. But being pregnant…it brings up lots of memories.

And the absence of certain memories.

"I would like to meet the father of my grandbaby," Mom says. "You will bring him over for dinner one day, okay?"

I am so not ready for this. "Not yet. But sometime before the baby comes."

"I will make sure that it actually happens and you do not keep putting it off. Perhaps you will change your mind about him. He did offer to marry you, yes? And having a baby can make people change their ways."

I think of the enormous pregnancy book that Vince brought to my appointment, the way he trusted me to make my own decisions about my health but wanted to be there to support me.

The doorbell rings.

"It must be the sushi," Mom says. "I think you can eat the

tempura, gyoza, and cucumber rolls. Next time, I will cook, and I will make only foods you can eat."

We head into the hall, where Larry is taking the bags of sushi from the delivery man. When Larry puts everything down in the kitchen, he gives me a hug, and the rest of the family joins him—his son, his daughter, her wife, and their six-year-old daughter.

Yes, it's all going to be okay.

[11]
VINCE

"Can I tell you a secret?" I ask Evie.

She's sitting beside me on the couch. I take her gurgle as a yes.

"You're getting another cousin near the end of the year. You're going to be a Big Cousin and show her—or him—how to do all sorts of tricks, won't you?"

Apparently this is funny. Evie laughs.

Evie already has three cousins. Courtney's older brother has two kids, and her younger sister has a daughter, Hazel, who is only nine days older than Evie. Courtney and her sister Naomi got pregnant at the same time and had nearly identical due dates. Hazel was born a few days early, but Evie decided to take her time. Naomi brings Hazel over to Courtney and Julian's once or twice a week so her husband, who's a writer, can get some time alone to work. Julian bought a second crib and other things for when Naomi and Hazel visit. I think going through everything at the same time as her sister has been really great for Courtney.

I'm pretty sure Marissa doesn't have any siblings. She said it was just her and her mother when she was growing up.

But I'll be there for her. Being a family man sounds like the right kind of life for me now. It would solve the pesky feelings of uselessness that have plagued me for so long. I don't just want to see our baby a couple times a week; I want to see them every day. I want to change diapers in the middle of the night and carry the baby around in a carrier.

"And it's thanks to you!" I say to Evie.

I hand her a Sophie the Giraffe toy. She looks at it with curiosity then sticks the head in her mouth.

If it wasn't for Evie—if this had happened a year ago, say—I would have panicked at the idea of being a father.

But I've fallen in love with my niece, and I want this for myself, too.

In fact, I'm rather jealous of Julian, my staid older brother.

He was always the organized, responsible one. Growing up with Julian was annoying at times, though I did look up to him.

I never wanted to work at Fong Investments, but now he has a career, a wife, and a child, and that sounds rather nice.

The Vince Fong who sold his company for two hundred million, slept for two weeks, then did nothing but party, would be horrified.

But that isn't exactly me anymore.

And I do want to have more sex with Marissa—that's part of the appeal of this plan.

I don't know who I am now, but I do know what I want.

I'm working through books on babies and parenthood, making a list of things we'll need—crib, change table, that sort of stuff—as I go. I'll purchase the items soon, then show Marissa the room I've set aside.

I don't live in the ideal place for a baby. Julian and Courtney moved from Julian's old penthouse to a house in Rosedale when they got married, and I see Marissa and I raising our child in a house, too. Maybe something in midtown, where she lives now.

I pull out my phone, add "buy house" to my list of things to do, then set it aside and turn my attention back to Evie. "How about we sing a song?" I kneel on the floor in front of the couch and start singing "I'm a Little Teapot."

She looks at me in confusion as I sing the first line, then starts crying when I hold up my handle and spout. She throws Sophie onto the cushions and wails at the top of her lungs.

Oh, dear.

I go back to our reliable favorite, "There Was an Old Woman Who Swallowed a Fly," but she doesn't like that, either.

I gather her up in my arms and walk around the playroom as I bounce. She was fed and changed before Courtney went up to have a shower, so I don't think it's either of those things.

Finally, I pick up a T-Rex puppet, which I got her before Julian instituted the no-presents-for-Evie rule.

"Raar," the T-rex says as it bites Evie's foot.

Somehow, this is less terrifying than me singing "I'm a Little Teapot."

She smiles.

"Does Evie like dinosaurs?" I ask.

In response, she makes some inarticulate noises.

"Dinosaurs were biiiig and scaaaary," I say, "but Evie's not scared, is she? She's a tough little girl."

The dinosaur—out of its own accord; I have nothing to do with this, of course—bites Evie's earlobe, which she finds even more amusing than when the dinosaur bit her foot.

"Oh, no. Where did your ear go, Evie? The dinosaur took it! Maybe you should be scared of dinosaurs after all."

The dinosaur opens his mouth and returns her earlobe.

"Wow, isn't that nice of him. He returned your ear. Let me sew it on." I mime stitching her ear together with one hand. "Uncle Vince is a hero, isn't he? He stitched your ear back on like a very competent surgeon."

The doorbell rings. Cedric said he might stop by today, so I head to the door. Sure enough, it's my brother.

"Hey, Evie." He shakes her little foot.

"Sing 'I'm a Little Teapot.' She likes it."

Cedric raises his eyebrows but dutifully starts singing as he takes off his shoes. Since when did my brother do what I ask?

"Man, you have a terrible voice," I say. "Look, you're making her cry!"

It's true, Evie is wailing. So it's not just my singing that upsets her today. Good to know.

The results of this experiment, however, may not be reproducible. Who knows what she'll like tomorrow.

To cheer Evie up, the dinosaur decides it's the perfect time to bite her little toes. She giggles in delight.

"You're so good with her." Cedric sounds a little deflated. "Do you want to be a dad?"

It's a good thing I wasn't drinking anything because I would have spit it all over him.

Actually, I'm going to be a dad later this year.

It's hard to keep that to myself, but Marissa made me promise not to tell anyone yet.

"Maybe, one day," I say nonchalantly. "Right now, I'm too busy having fun and jetting around the world."

"You really haven't done much traveling lately."

"I went to New York City."

"That was a while ago. And you seem to be in bed by three in the morning these days. No partying until the sun rises."

"Getting old, you know." I don't particularly like being questioned about my life, so I turn the tables. "Do *you* want to be a father?"

Evie takes this opportunity to touch my face. Her hand is a little slobbery, but I've gotten used to slobbery baby hands and it doesn't bother me. She's definitely gotten grabbier in the last few weeks, though.

Cedric still seems to be pondering my question.

"No," he says at last.

I'm tempted to say that he'll change his mind one day, but that's stupid. Not everyone wants the same things in life.

"I wasn't sure," Cedric said, "and I thought maybe Evie would help me figure it out. And she's fun and all…" He lightly covers her ears. "In small doses. I see what Courtney and Julian have to do for her and think, 'God, no.'"

"Fair enough." I swallow the rest of my words, about how I want to be part of a child's everyday life. Not gonna lie, I think I'll cry the first time my child calls me "dada."

That condom failing was the best thing that happened to me in a long time.

But Marissa Chan—yes, I know her last name!—just wants me as her baby's father. For now. I'm still hoping I can change her mind and we'll have a happy family life together.

Evie sticks her little fingers in my mouth, and I nibble them.

"Oh, no! Where did your fingers go? Should I stitch them back on?"

Instead of suddenly figuring out how to answer yes or no questions, Evie shoves her whole hand in my mouth, and this is a little weird, but if she's having fun—

"Oh my fucking God!"

That shriek is me.

Holy shit. That hurt.

I pull Evie's hand out of my mouth and pass her over to Cedric so I can curl up in a ball and whimper.

Okay, that's not quite what I do, but it's easier to nurse my pain without a baby in my arms. Especially a bloodthirsty baby like Evie.

"What happened?" Cedric asks, and I can tell he's holding back laughter. The bastard.

"She scratched the roof of my mouth with all five of those sharp little claws."

Evie smiles, as though pleased with her accomplishment.

"Don't worry, I still love you," I say.

She lets out a whopper of a fart in response, and given how Cedric is holding her, the smell goes directly into his nose. He makes a disgusted face. Before he can put her down, she farts again, extra moist.

Now it's my turn to laugh. "Yeah, I really love you, Evie. I forgive you for all the stitches I'm going to need. Always fart in Uncle Cedric's face, okay?"

"Do you think she pooped?" Cedric asks. "We should find Courtney."

"Nah, I can change a diaper."

"You've done it before?"

"A few times, yes."

Soon, this will be a regular occurrence in my life.

I'm okay with that.

That evening, rather than changing poopy diapers, I'm living the Vince Fong lifestyle.

I'm wearing a three-piece suit—I think I look particularly fine in a three-piece suit, if I do say so myself—and sitting in the lounge of a fancy Financial District restaurant with Brian Poon. The restaurant is on the forty-second floor, so we have a nice view of the city at night.

I met Brian when I came back to Toronto after selling my company. He was also young and rich and not terribly busy, plus he hosted great parties. We started hanging out regularly.

Brian takes a sip of his very expensive whiskey—he has ridiculously posh tastes, whereas I'm not quite as picky—and glances again at the trim white guy in the corner. The man is casually dressed for a venue like this, though I bet that sweater wasn't cheap.

"Just go talk to him already," I say. "You're undressing him with your eyes."

"We need to find a lady for you first."

"Nah, I've had enough sex lately." A lie, but I will not be picking up a woman tonight.

"Not interested at all?" Brian frowns. "Is something wrong with your dick?"

"Nothing's wrong. Just don't feel like picking up tonight."

My friend looks at me like I have three heads. "What about that lady in the red-sequined dress by the window?" He tilts his head toward a South Asian woman.

I picture Marissa wearing the same dress.

I picture that dress pushed down around her waist, her tits bare and her legs wrapped around me.

It's a lovely thought.

Yeah, when I jack off in the shower now, it's always to thoughts of her.

"No, I'm fine," I say.

Brian appears truly concerned. "I can't leave you alone when you're down like this."

"I'm not down. I'm doing just fine." I smile at him.

"That's your fake smile."

"No, it's not." I smile wider.

"Definitely your fake smile." He glances toward the corner once more. The man has his eyes on Brian now.

My phone buzzes and I immediately reach for it. I have a text from Marissa.

You busy?

I feel a genuine smile coming to my lips.

"Booty call?" Brian asks.

"Something like that. You go have your fun."

Brian leans forward and looks at me for a long moment. I think he's going to say something else, but he shrugs and saunters off.

Nope, I reply to Marissa. *Not busy.*

Then I realize that if she's texting me, it might mean something's wrong.

Shit.

I stare at my phone, fearful as I wait for her reply.

I'm having some cravings, she says.

Oh, thank God.

For me? I ask, though I knew that's not when she means.

No, you self-absorbed asshole.

I laugh.

I'm craving some very specific foods, and I was wondering if you could get them for me. You at home?

Excellent. I can be useful for once!

Nah, but I'm close, I reply.

But you're not busy?

The guy I'm with is trying to pick up. And as I said, I'd like you to tell me whenever you need anything. Don't worry about my exciting life. What do you want?

Matcha double fromage cheesecake from Cheese & Me, she says. *Plus beef and celery dumplings from Yang's Dumplings. You know the places?*

Yep. I'll bring you the food as soon as I can.

I unfold myself from my chair. The woman in the red dress slides her gaze over my body, but I just wave at Brian, who looks up briefly, and head out.

Cheese & Me is a popular Japanese cheesecake place downtown, fortunately quite close to where I am. I jump into the car that's waiting for me and tell the driver where to go.

When I arrive five minutes later, it's packed with people enjoying cheesecake and cheese tarts. The line-up is long, and I try not to tap my foot as I wait.

Finally, it's my turn.

"One matcha double fromage cheesecake," I say.

"I'm sorry," the woman says. "We just sold our last one."

Another server deposits what I'm pretty sure is a matcha

double fromage cheesecake into a box. He hands it to the man beside me. Goddammit.

"But we do have our regular matcha cheesecake," the woman suggests. "Really, it's quite good."

I turn to the man. "I'll pay you double for that cheesecake."

He shakes his head. "This is for my mother. It's her birthday tomorrow."

"Triple," I say, but it's half-hearted. I'd feel like a monster, taking the cake he picked out for his mom's birthday. Surely there's some amount of money that would make him cave, but I'm not going to try to find it.

"Tempting, but no. Look, there's a place that's almost as good, and it also does double fromage cheesecakes. It's on Dundas."

But Marissa said the matcha double fromage cheesecake from Cheese & Me, and I'm determined to get exactly what she wants.

I turn back to the server. "Okay, I'll get a regular matcha cheesecake." Just in case my plan doesn't work out.

After she boxes up the cheesecake for me, I walk around the crowded seating area, trying to see if anyone has a matcha double fromage cheesecake. There's a group of teenage girls in the corner with one, but they've already finished most of it.

The young couple at the back, however, is more promising. They each have a slice of cheesecake on their plates, but more than half the cheesecake is left, and it looks like they haven't touched it with their forks.

I approach their table. "I'll give you twenty bucks for the rest of your cheesecake."

The girl looks at me suspiciously. "Why don't you buy your own?"

"They ran out."

"What's the catch?" the guy asks. "Surely they have lots of other things you could buy. Why don't you get a cheese tart?"

"I don't want a cheese tart. I want a matcha double fromage cheesecake, and you two have about sixty percent of one, which is good enough. I can give you half of my regular matcha cheese-cake, too."

"As well as thirty bucks?" the girl asks.

"He said twenty," the guy hisses across the table. "The cake cost us twenty-two bucks. Twenty for what's left is a good deal."

"He seems pretty desperate. Might as well try to get more money out of him."

The guy looks at the girl like she just said the smartest thing he's ever heard. They get lost in each other's eyes for a moment.

"So, do we have a deal?" I say impatiently.

"Why do you want the cake so badly?" the girl asks. I figure they're about nineteen—students at one of the nearby universities, perhaps.

"My wife is pregnant and she's craving it."

It sounds better to say "my wife" instead of "the woman I knocked up."

"And she'll probably be really disappointed if you don't bring it home. She might make you sleep in the spare room for the week. You *really* need this cake, don't you?"

I roll my eyes.

"Look, Vi," the guy says. "Thirty bucks is good. Don't force him to pay a ridiculous sum for a half-eaten cake."

"Why not? He's wearing a three-piece suit. I'm sure he can afford it. Who the hell wears a three-piece suit?"

"Most women find it sexy," I say defensively.

"And why are you even thinking about any woman but your wife?"

I don't know how a simple conversation got so far off the rails.

"Forty bucks." She crosses her arms over her chest.

"Fine," I say. "Forty it is."

I take out the box with the matcha cheesecake. I use a knife from their table to cut it 60/40, then switch the larger piece with their matcha double fromage cheesecake. I don't know what on earth a double fromage cheesecake is, but it's what Marissa wants, and that's all that matters. Then I place two twenties on the table.

"Thank you," I say. "My wife will be very happy."

"You're a sucker," the girl says. "I would have given it to you for thirty."

I'm tempted to make some asshole comment about how much money I have, but I let it go. As I head to the door, I hear the guy say, "What a weirdo."

Well, whatever. This weirdo now has sixty percent of a matcha double fromage cheesecake and forty percent of a matcha cheesecake, which will hopefully be enough to make a pregnant woman very happy.

I jump into the car waiting a block away, and I'm about to tell my driver to head to Marissa's building when I remember the rest of her request.

Beef and celery dumplings. Right.

Hopefully this will be easier than the cheesecake.

[12]

MARISSA

CRAVINGS ARE WEIRD.

Earlier this week, I craved salted caramel ice cream. And pretzels. Every night, as soon as I got home from work, I'd serve myself a small bowl of salted caramel ice cream with crushed pretzels on top. I'd sigh in bliss when I slid the spoon into my mouth.

It was as good as an orgasm.

Then today, I got a sudden craving for matcha cheesecake. But not just any matcha cheesecake. No, the matcha double fromage cheesecake at Cheese & Me.

This presented a problem. Cheese & Me is downtown, and I do not live downtown. And it's Friday night, and I did not want to head downtown just to eat cheesecake.

But dammit, I really wanted that cheesecake.

Vince said I could text him if I needed anything, so I decided to take him up on that offer. I also asked him to get me some dumplings, which I'm not exactly *craving*, but they sounded really good to me, and why not? The dumpling place is near Cheese & Me.

I just buzzed him in, so my cheesecake will be here any minute. My mouth is watering.

There's a knock on the door. I'm standing right next to it—yes, I'm that excited—so I open it right up.

"Did you get everything?" I ask, suddenly worried he failed in his mission.

"Yep." Vince hands me two bags, then takes off his shoes and coat, and oh my God, he's wearing a three-piece gray suit underneath.

My mouth is *really* watering now.

"What were you doing tonight?" I ask.

"Just having a drink at a lounge."

"You certainly drink at fancier places than I do. Than I used to, I mean. I'm not drinking anymore." I don't want him to think I'm endangering the health of his baby.

I carry the bags into the kitchen and take out the Cheese & Me box. What greets me when I open the lid is a surprise. He has indeed gotten me matcha double fromage cheesecake—a generous half of one. There's also a smaller half of a different cheesecake.

I don't understand, but I don't care. I grab a fork and stab my beloved double fromage cheesecake. When I put the first bite in my mouth, I moan.

"Good?" Vince asks.

I don't answer. I'm too busy shoveling cheesecake into my mouth.

I eat a third of it before I look at Vince again. His lips are quirked up. He hasn't shaved in a few days, and it works well on him.

"Explain this situation." I gesture at the box of cheesecake with my fork. "Why are there two different cheesecakes?"

"They had just sold the last matcha double fromage cheese-cake to another man. I tried to buy it off him for triple the price, but he refused—it's for his mother's birthday. So, I bought a regular matcha cheesecake, then walked around the room until I found a couple with your desired cheesecake who were willing to part with what they had left. I gave them forty bucks and part of my cheesecake for it. They drove a hard bargain, but I wasn't going to turn up without any matcha double fromage cheesecake from Cheese & Me."

Oh my God. This man.

I drop my fork and kiss him.

He's caught off-guard, but then his arms come around me and he kisses me back. I cup his slightly-scruffy jaw and slide my tongue between his lips. He tastes of liquor—I'm not sure what kind, but I bet it's expensive—and some kind of spice. It's perfect. At least as good as my matcha double fromage cheesecake, and isn't that a disturbing thought, since a minute ago I was thinking that cheesecake was the pinnacle of human achievement. His mouth is warm and welcoming, and we meld together just right.

At last, I step back and return to the cheesecake.

"Uh, sorry," I say, somewhat sheepishly. "I don't know what came over me."

He puts his finger under my chin and tilts my head up. "I think you do."

"Fine. You're really fucking handsome in that suit. What is it about three-piece suits? They look so good and I rarely see men our age wear them. You also brought me that magnificent cheesecake—"

"And you were helpless to resist me. Got it. Kind of like the time you walked up to me at a party and shoved my hand up your skirt."

"That's not quite what happened."

"If you want to do it again, I'd be agreeable."

"Must be tough for you to go without sex since you promised to be faithful to me, even though I didn't ask for it. But the answer is no."

I'm slightly tempted, but I have self-restraint.

I return to scarfing down the cheesecake.

"Out of curiosity," he says, "what is this double fromage cheesecake?"

"It's a thin layer of matcha sponge cake, followed by baked matcha cheesecake with some kind of creamy mousse on top—that's the white layer. Not too sweet, but so delicious."

"And what's the green coating? It looks like AstroTurf."

"Hey, it looks much more appealing than AstroTurf. It's crumbled matcha sponge cake." I hesitate. I'm not sure I want to do this, but he did come all this way. "Want to try a bite?"

"You're offering me a bite? How generous."

"It's extremely generous. If you'd managed to get me an entire matcha double fromage cheesecake, I might have offered you more than a bite."

"They'd run out!"

"I'm teasing. I can't believe you paid someone forty bucks for half a small cheesecake."

"It was a young couple. They could probably use the money. And they said my suit was ridiculous."

I gasp. "How shocking."

I pick up a bite of cheesecake with my fork, careful to get all the layers. I hold it up to his mouth, and he eats it.

Feeding him is painfully intimate.

It reminds me of when we ate cold pizza during our infamous weekend together.

"The cheesecake is good," he says quietly, "and it was worth all the trouble to get it for you." He slides his hand through my hair, pushing it back from my face.

"Man, you're really putting the moves on me."

"What can I say? It's what I do." He has an odd expression—there's a hint of sadness in it. "But I promise I'm not putting these moves on anyone else. Just the mother of my child."

Against my will, my inner muscles clench. The thought of being *his* is annoyingly appealing. He says he hasn't been with anyone else, and maybe it's foolish, but I believe him.

I put down my fork once I've eaten half the double fromage cheesecake. "I should stop. I just remembered that matcha has caffeine—I was so focused on my craving that I forgot about that —and you're not supposed to overdo it on caffeine when you're pregnant. I'll have the rest tomorrow."

"None for me?"

"You can have the other cheesecake."

"Very generous," he murmurs. "You want your dumplings now?" He takes them out of the bag. "Two orders of beef and celery for you. And me, if you don't want them all, but I also got some pork ones for myself. I'll have my cheesecake after my dumplings. That's the proper way to do things."

I snort. "You're calling yourself proper?"

"Mmm. Very proper."

Ugh, why is that seductive tone of his so damn effective on me?

He grins. He knows what he's done.

We eat our dumplings in silence for a few minutes. It's a bit surreal. It's ten o'clock at night, and I'm eating dumplings at my kitchen table with a really hot man in a suit, while I'm pregnant and craving weird things and dressed in pajama pants and a ratty long-sleeve shirt.

He kissed me back.

It sends a thrill down my spine.

My libido has been mostly absent since I discovered I was pregnant, in part because of the morning sickness, but tonight…

Nope, not happening.

We finish our dumplings, and he cuts himself a modest slice of matcha cheesecake.

"Look at you, trying to be all proper," I mutter. "Actually cutting a slice rather than just stabbing the cake with your fork."

He smiles, then shifts the knife to the double fromage cheese-cake and mimes cutting off a piece.

"Don't you dare," I say. "I'll want that tomorrow."

He laughs. "You know I was teasing."

"Don't joke about stuff like that. This is serious business."

He leans forward, and I think he's about to take my hand, but he doesn't. Stupidly, I'm disappointed. "Do you need anything from me other than dumplings and cheesecake delivery?"

"No, I'm doing okay. Other than the morning sickness—it's not as terrible as some women have it, I know—and my aversion to mushrooms, it's not too bad. I can feel my body changing, though. Like, my bras don't fit right anymore."

Maybe I shouldn't have said that. It's weird talking about bras with Vince, isn't it?

Our relationship—it's weird.

Having a baby within a marriage would be much more straightforward. But we're not in love, and we're not getting married.

"I told my mom," I say. "I didn't mean for Larry's children to find out too, but they did, because I looked like a deer caught in headlights when I learned we were having sushi for dinner and Larry offered me a glass of wine."

"Who's Larry?"

"My mom's husband."

Vince doesn't ask any more questions, for which I'm thankful. At some point, I'll tell him more about my family, but not yet.

"My mom wants to meet you," I say. "At some point before the baby arrives, can you come over for dinner?"

"Sure. My parents will probably want to meet you, too, if that's okay. I haven't told them yet, don't worry. At twelve weeks, right?"

"Yes."

"My brother asked if I wanted to be a dad, and it was tough to keep a straight face."

"I'm sorry."

"Don't be. I understand wanting to wait until the second

trimester. It's not a problem." He stuffs some cheesecake in his mouth. "This one is just as good, you know."

"No, the double fromage cheesecake is better." I pop the last dumpling in my mouth with my chopsticks, then pick up another bite of the double fromage cheesecake with my fork. I hold it to his lips.

"A second bite? Wow, you really are generous."

"Shut your mouth. I mean, open it. So I can put the cheese-cake in."

He does as I request.

"The problem is that you didn't taste them one after the other before," I say. "But now you have, and you agree the so-called AstroTurf one is better, don't you?"

He ponders this for a moment. "No, I like them equally."

"You're just saying that to piss me off."

"I'm telling you the truth."

"You're a monster." I shake my head. "A kind, *generous* monster who went out of his way to get this pregnant lady what she wanted."

"It's no trouble. Really, Marissa, I don't mind."

This time, he does take my hand in his and looks at me intently.

My face feels like it's on fire.

"Uh, thanks for everything," I say, "but I'm tired and you should probably be going. Get back to your three-piece-suit-wearing friends or whatever it is while I go to bed."

He stands up. "Sure."

I shouldn't be annoyed that he's doing what I told him to do, but I am. Though I'm also relieved.

I'm relieved, aren't I?

Despite his ridiculous proposal when I told him I was pregnant, Vince has been good at not intruding in my life where I don't want him, but still being there when I ask.

And he's a hell of a good kisser and wears that suit so well it would make angels weep.

God, that kiss…

I press my fingertips to my mouth before standing up and walking him to the door.

"See you soon," I say. "At the ultrasound, if nothing else."

"If you develop any cravings you want me to satisfy, be sure to let me know." He winks.

"Vince—"

"Like, say, you really want some har gow. Or aloo gobi. Or Portuguese egg tarts. Anything like that. Why, what were you thinking?"

I fix him with my death glare. "Go, Vince."

"Alright, I'm going."

But before he does, he presses a quick kiss to my cheek.

I clean up the kitchen and write out my grocery list for tomorrow—definitely need to stock up on salted caramel ice cream and pretzels—and that kiss lingers.

What will Vince do now? He said his friend was trying to pick up, but surely he has other things to do this Friday night. Parties to attend, exclusive night clubs to check out?

If I'd asked him to stay to watch a movie and snuggle up on the couch…would he have?

Vince and I are now stuck in each other's lives, but even though I'm attracted to him, I'm not going to make out with him again. We're going to be co-parents; that's what is important, and I can't imagine us actually being together, even if he feels otherwise. At this point, anything physical would just complicate matters.

Next time, I will control my urges. I blame my little slip-up on pregnancy hormones and that mouth-watering suit.

Sure, the man who got me pregnant is hot, but I can resist him. No problem.

Ha.

~

Saturday afternoon, I head to an independent coffee shop on Mount Pleasant and order a London fog. A few minutes later, Pearl Liang orders a latte and sits down across from me.

I've known Pearl for years. We used to hang out all the time, but now she has two small children and a full-time job, and it's hard to coordinate our schedules.

It's so good to see her for the first time in months. I give her a hug.

She tilts her head. "You look different. New haircut?"

"No." I pause. "I'm pregnant. Maybe that's it."

"You're pregnant." Her eyes widen, but when I smile at her, she smiles back. We hug again. "Congratulations. Wow, I really am out of the loop. Who's the guy you're seeing?"

"I'm not seeing anyone. Just a guy I spent a night—okay, two nights—with. Apparently, our birth control failed, and here I am. Pregnant."

"Not that there's anything wrong with it, but I never imagined you having a child outside of a relationship. You used to talk about wanting a two-parent family for your child."

"The father will still be involved, which is important to me. But I'm getting old, and I'd like a kid. I need to be flexible."

"If you're happy," she says, squeezing my hand, "then I'm happy. Have you told your mother?"

"Yeah. It took her a minute to wrap her mind around it, but it was fine. She's already sewing baby clothes."

"If you have any questions about pregnancy, you know you can ask me, anytime. And since I'm officially done having kids, I have lots of things I don't need anymore that I could give you. Like a baby bouncer."

"That would be great."

We talk for a while about pregnancy and her children—and what little adorable devils they are—until she says, "Okay, I have to ask. Who's the father? You say he's going to be involved, so I assume this isn't a big secret. Do I know him?"

"No, but you might know *of* him. Vince Fong."

"The name does sound familiar. Oh, is he Charles Fong's son?"

"Yeah. The youngest one. The tech start-up guy."

"He's known for being, uh, quite popular with women, right?"

"Yep, and I fell for his charms." And then I kissed him again last night. "But he's really not so bad, and he was pretty excited when I told him about the pregnancy."

"Marissa," Pearl says, her voice laced with amusement.

Oh, God, I know that voice.

"Are you falling for him, maybe a little?"

"No," I scoff.

She gives me a look.

This is the problem with knowing someone for more than two decades. She can read me too well.

"Well, he's really hot," I admit.

"I think I need to see what this man looks like." Pearl pulls out her phone, and not much later, she lets out a low whistle. "He does look quite nice without a shirt."

"What pictures are you looking at?" I grab the phone from her hand. I only have memories of what he looks like shirtless. Pictures would be nice.

I'm sure he'd take his shirt off for me if I asked, but I wouldn't be able to stand his infuriating smirk.

The picture Pearl has pulled up is from a calendar, several years old now. I'll have to tease him about this.

And yeah, he looks good, a cocky smile on his face, but something bothers me about his expression. I zoom in. Maybe if I'd never been up close and personal with him, I wouldn't be able to tell, but he looks…exhausted. Like he's barely holding it together.

"You haven't Googled him before?" Pearl asks. "You would have easily found this photo if you had."

"No, I was afraid of what I might find."

"You're having his kid, though."

I sip my London fog. "Why did it have to be him? Why couldn't one of the guys I actually dated have gotten me pregnant?"

"Well…" Pearl says.

"Right. One of them did."

Sanjay went to the clinic with me and held my hand. *One day, he said, we'll have a baby together. When the time is right.*

But that didn't happen. We broke up several months later. The relationship was comfortable and safe, but I didn't love him enough.

This is an unfortunate pattern with me. I meet a respectable and genuinely nice guy. Usually, I'm the one who makes the first move. We date for a while, maybe we exchange "I love yous." Occasionally, he ends it, but usually I get bored and end it first.

I have no history of going for assholes who break my heart.

Sanjay got married five years ago and has a few kids. I don't talk to him anymore, but we're "friends" on Facebook, and I like when a picture pops up of him with his family. He always looks happy, and I'm glad for him.

Then I inevitably get a little sad. Why can't I have what he has?

Maybe I should have "settled" for one of my exes. Have I been looking for the impossible, for a love that doesn't exist?

No, I don't think so. I think I've just been unlucky and haven't met the right guy yet.

"If you have a little crush on Vince," Pearl says, "it's probably because he's a sweetheart, underneath everything else. You have impeccable taste in men. Unlike me."

"You're the one who's married."

"But until my husband, I was doing pretty poorly with dating. You're different."

"Why couldn't I really, truly love one of those guys?" I shake my head, frustrated with myself, but there's no point in dwelling on it. "The reason I'm not letting myself fall for Vince is because I know he's all wrong. He's definitely not a sweetheart."

I remember what happened the night we met.

Nope, definitely not sweet.

Then last night…

"You're blushing!" Pearl says.

"Pregnancy hormones," I mutter.

"Or…"

I have another sip of my drink. "Last night he brought me matcha double fromage cheesecake because I was craving it." I don't bother describing how hot he looked when he delivered my food. That image is just for me.

"From Cheese & Me?"

"Yeah."

We both spend the next minute salivating.

If I was a truly good friend, I might have brought her the small piece I have left, but I'm keeping that for myself.

I mean, I'm pregnant. I deserve it.

"I'm just saying," Pearl says, "maybe don't write off the cute guy who brings you cheesecake."

"You're a romantic, wanting me to have a happy nuclear family."

She shrugs. "Perhaps you need someone who's a little different from the other men you've been with. Now tell me." She leans forward. "Does he really look that good without a shirt, or are the pictures lying?"

I laugh. "No, they're not lying."

As I walk home, I wonder if maybe Pearl has a point.

[13]

VINCE

I STAND on the balcony—one of many balconies—at Brian's house and look out at his backyard. The sun has set, but there are enough lights for me to make out the edge of the tennis court and hedge maze.

It's late March, and I'm a little cold in my suit jacket, though the whiskey warms me from the inside. The music and sounds of the party reach my ears, but I just stand here, sipping my drink.

"Hey, Vince." Alexis saunters up to me.

I force a smile for her. "Hey. How are you?"

"I'd prefer to do a little less talking," she says, sliding her hand up my arm.

I immediately stiffen.

She pulls back.

"Sorry," I say. "Just not in the mood today."

She looks at me like I said the earth is flat or something equally absurd, but she doesn't push it.

I don't blame her for her reaction. I'm acting pretty out of character.

But I made a promise to Marissa, and to be honest, it's not a difficult promise to keep. When I think of her wearing those frayed purple pajamas and stuffing cheesecake into her mouth—and then kissing me—it's hard to want anyone else.

"What are you drinking?" I ask Alexis.

"I have no idea, but it's delicious! That bartender is amazing. You tell her a few cocktails or ingredients you like, and she makes something up on the spot. Want to try?" She holds out her glass.

Sharing drinks has never bothered me, but now, all I can imagine is getting sick and passing it along to Marissa and harming the baby and...

I shake my head. "No, I'm fine."

We talk for a few more minutes about the party before Alexis heads back inside. I return to staring out at the yard and drinking in silence.

The silence doesn't last long, however.

"Vince! I didn't believe it when I heard you were brooding on the balcony, but it's true."

I turn and see Holden Khoo, and my face splits into a grin.

"Holden." I slap him on the back. "Good to see you."

He turns to Brian. "He doesn't seem unhappy."

"But he hasn't been himself lately," Brian says.

I don't claim I'm just the same as always, because that's not true. My regular life doesn't hold my interest.

Although it's still good to see my friends.

I met Holden through Brian, and we've been friends for a while. He lives in Vancouver, but he comes to Toronto on a regular basis.

"I didn't know you were visiting this weekend," I say to him.

"I did tell you," Brian says. "When you arrived tonight. But you were spaced out again, and totally ignoring the girl who was hitting on you. Speaking of that, Gabriella and I were going to..." He waggles his eyebrows. "You want to join? Like last time?"

Yes, Brian and I have fucked the same girl before. A bunch of times, in fact.

"Not tonight," I say.

I imagine what I'd tell Marissa. *Sorry, honey, I had to break my promise to you. My friends were getting too suspicious, and I didn't want to say anything before twelve weeks. So I had a threesome at a party, no big deal.*

No, I'm not tempted.

"Seriously, man," Brian says. "I'm worried about you."

"I'm fine, I promise."

Brian places his hand on my arm. "You're acting weird, and it's been that way for a while. You can't deny it. You're not acting like *Vince Fong.*"

But who's the Vince Fong that the world sees? A useless playboy with a penthouse and lots of money. A guy who just cares about having fun.

It sort of disgusts me that I'm nothing more than that.

Though it's not like all my relationships with people are shallow, superficial things. Sure, I goof off around my family, and I'm particularly fond of getting on Julian's nerves, but that's just the way I express love sometimes. And I'm utterly enamored with my baby niece. Just the thought that soon I'll have a baby myself makes me smile.

Me and Marissa and a baby and a little house. The meaning I've been missing.

Holden peers at me curiously. "I know what happened. Vince has fallen in love."

"No, that's not it," I say, and it's not a lie.

I'm very fond of Marissa, it's true. I think we'd work well together. But it would be an exaggeration to say that I love her. Not yet. I expect I'll come to love her, though—she's pretty amazing, after all—and I desperately hope she'll return my feelings.

Or is it not possible for someone to feel that way about me?

I shove down my doubts.

Brian stares at me as he drums his fingers on the railing.

"Okay, fine," I say. "Something *is* up with me. It's not bad, don't worry. I have to keep it a secret for now, but I'll tell you soon, I promise."

Brian and Holden glance at each other.

"Maybe it's a new business deal," Holden says, "and it's making him a little anxious because he's been out of the tech world for a while."

I never want to go back to that life. It nearly destroyed me, and what would be the purpose? Just to give myself something to occupy my time? I have no drive to do it again.

But I don't feel like saying all that to my friends, so I just shrug.

"Yeah, maybe that's it," Brian says. "Still, his actions don't make sense."

Now I understand how aggravated Julian must feel when Cedric and I talk about him in his presence. My friends are getting on my nerves, but I just grit my teeth.

Even if I did tell them the truth, would they understand?

I'm so weary of it all.

How many zillion parties have I attended in the past few years? While Julian has been falling in love and getting married and having a child…and also buying a phallic cactus named Joey and learning to bake?

Just then, my phone buzzes, and I smile when I see it's Marissa.

I'm craving a matcha double fromage cheesecake again.

"Yeah, he's definitely in love," Holden says.

"Vince, in love? I hope not." Brian shakes his head. "No, I'm going for the business deal. He just got good news."

"Sorry, guys, I have to take off." I put my hand on Holden's shoulder. "Good to see you again. You staying in town for a few days?"

"Yep."

"Come over tomorrow, okay? I'll be around. There's a great brunch place that opened up around the corner from me."

He looks at me like I've sprouted three heads.

I laugh. "Just kidding about brunch. But come by sometime, okay?"

I head downstairs and outside, and I tell my driver to take me to Cheese & Me. The Bridle Path isn't a long drive from Marissa's condo, but I have to go downtown to get her cheesecake first. By some miracle, Cheese & Me actually has a matcha double fromage cheesecake at ten thirty at night, so I don't have to find someone who will allow me to overpay for half of theirs. Excellent.

Marissa answers the door in pajamas again, but different ones this time. The pants are pink with stars, and her T-shirt says "pregnant and hungry."

I laugh.

"What's so funny?" she asks, narrowing her eyes.

"Your shirt."

"Right. I forgot about that. Were you able to get the cheesecake?"

She holds out her hands, and I pass it over.

"Oh my God. Thank you."

She brings it into the kitchen, and just like last time, she starts ravenously eating the cheesecake with a plastic fork while I look on, amused.

"What were you doing when I texted?" she asks between bites.

"I was at a party."

She immediately stops eating. "Sorry. You could have stayed. I wasn't craving cheesecake *that* badly."

I pointedly look at the cheesecake.

"Okay, fine, but you don't have to answer to my every whim. The fact that I'm pregnant doesn't mean you can't enjoy life."

"I wasn't enjoying myself all that much at the party, to be honest. I'm glad you gave me an excuse to leave."

"Not enough drugs and sex for you?"

"I had two whiskeys. No sex. My life isn't quite what you

imagine."

I'm not sure she hears what I'm saying, as her focus is on the cheesecake.

Once she's eaten about twenty percent of it, she finally makes eye contact with me. "Thank you. For bringing me cheesecake again." She looks me up and down. "The three-piece suit was a little hotter, I have to admit."

"The navy two-piece suit isn't good enough for you?"

"Oh, you still look pretty hot, don't you worry."

"Hot enough for you to kiss me again?" I say, before I can give it a second thought.

She considers this for a long moment.

She's driving me nuts.

And then, instead of speaking, she presses a slow kiss to my lips. When I lick her bottom lip, she eagerly dives in for more, and my cock hardens.

I didn't feel anywhere near this alive at the party.

We kiss for a few minutes, and then she decides she needs a little more cheesecake.

Once she's got the cheesecake in the fridge, she says, hesitantly, "You want to stay and watch a movie?"

"Yes," I reply, without asking which movie she plans to watch.

It ends up being a thriller with lots of white dudes who all look the same, and when I say this to Marissa, she laughs harder than is warranted and puts her arm around me. She snuggles up even closer during a particularly thrilling chase scene, where one white dude with short hair is being pursued by a pack of white dudes with short hair through a city.

I'm not paying much attention. I'm more focused on Marissa, her body pressed against mine. This isn't the way I usually spend my Friday nights. A quiet evening snuggling, eating cheesecake, and watching a movie is not what I'm known for.

But you know what? I could use more of this.

As long as it's with Marissa.

[14]

MARISSA

I'VE MADE it to twelve weeks. Yay!

Apparently the fetus is now the size of a plum, and I found myself looking at plums in an odd way when I was at the grocery store this morning.

Today I'm having my first ultrasound. Vince is supposed to accompany me. He should pick me up from my condo in five minutes, and I'm not worried that he'll show up.

Sure enough, he arrives right on time, and we make it to the ultrasound clinic fifteen minutes early. I check in and we take a seat in the waiting area. Across from us is a young couple, their hands intertwined. The woman has an engagement ring on her left hand, plus a wedding band, and she's further along than me. I'm guessing they're both about twenty-five.

I suddenly feel old.

Is it crazy to be pregnant at thirty-six with a man I hardly know?

But I've gotten to know Vince a little better in the past few weeks. We've seen each other a bunch of times. We've eaten cheesecake together. (Well, okay, I ate most of the cheesecake.) We've watched a movie together.

And on Wednesday, I did something terrible.

When I got home from work, I was exhausted but also filled with an unbearable loneliness, which has happened a bunch of times in the past few years.

So, I told Vince I was craving Thai basil chicken.

I was not, in fact, craving anything.

Don't get me wrong, Thai basil chicken definitely sounded good. It wasn't a pregnancy craving, though.

However, I pretended it was, and Vince picked some up and drove to my condo, and we ate together at my kitchen table. This time, he wasn't wearing a suit, just jeans and a sweater.

Today, he's not dressed up fancy, either. He's wearing a gray Henley, and he looks pretty hot in it, as I'm sure he knows. I'm not going to tell him and inflate his ego even more.

But though I appreciate his good looks, I can't say I'm turned on. I'm feeling a touch nauseous, and to be honest, I'm envious of the kids sitting across from us.

They're married, and they're having a baby together. How did they manage to get everything in order at such a young age? My generation is getting married and buying houses and having kids at lower rates, aren't we? We're alternately blamed for spending too much money and killing industries because we're not spending enough.

I live by myself, and I own property in an expensive city, and I feel like I'm doing well.

But these kids have something I don't.

Her ring is small, but who cares? I wouldn't want a big rock. Her husband whispers something in her ear, then puts his hand on her slightly-curved belly.

I imagine them living in a one-bedroom basement apartment and waking up with smiles on their faces each morning.

And here I am, single with a "geriatric" pregnancy. My body would probably handle pregnancy a little better if I was twenty-five. Maybe I wouldn't be so tired.

I take a deep breath. This isn't what I thought I'd have, but it's okay. It's not the life my mother imagined for me, either, but she's supportive.

"How are you doing?" Vince whispers, looking up from the book on pregnancy he's reading. It's a different one from last time. I haven't asked how many he's read.

"I'm fine," I say.

But although my body has been changing, waiting for the ultrasound makes everything seem more real than it did before.

"I'll take you out for something to eat after." He squeezes my hand. "Whatever you like."

"Okay." That sounds nice.

"Did you know the fetus is now as big as a lime?"

"My book says it's as big as a plum."

"Same difference, I guess." He pauses. "Though limes are more uniform in size than plums, aren't they? So maybe that's a better comparison."

"Are you trying to say your book is better than mine—"

My stomach objects to this conversation about plums and limes. I put my hand to my mouth, feeling like I'm about to hurl, and Vince grabs a garbage can.

Fortunately, the urge soon passes.

"You sure you're okay?" he asks.

"Yeah."

Across from us, the man is singing to his wife's stomach. "Rock-a-bye Baby," which is kind of a horrible song if you listen to the lyrics. In the background, a Katy Perry song is playing.

Then Everclear comes on.

"I like this one," I murmur.

"Yeah, it's a good song," Vince says.

Across from us, the mother-to-be exclaims, "Oh my God, I love classic rock!"

Classic rock? What the fuck?

Vince chuckles at the look of outrage on my face.

And then the man stops singing, and he and his wife discuss all the "classic" songs they like. I'm feeling more and more horrified by the second.

OMG, I really am old.

"I'm going to throw up!" I cry.

Vince thrusts the garbage can in front of me just in time.

I'm sitting on the exam table, feeling not too bad now. The ultrasound and a few other tests have been completed.

The ultrasound technician returns to the room with Vince, who stands beside me and squeezes my hand. The technician shows us the image on the screen and explains, roughly, what everything is. The results will be sent to my ob-gyn.

"It's cool, isn't it?" I say.

"Yeah." Vince's single-word response is quiet. "That's our baby-to-be."

There are tears on his cheeks, and something in my chest clenches. I wrap my arms around his waist.

"I can give you two a minute," the technician says.

"No, no," Vince says, "I want to hear the heartbeat. You can do that now, right?"

Yes. I waited for him, not wanting to hear it before he did. The ultrasound technician picks up the Doppler and places it on my stomach.

Soon, we hear it.

"Wow." Vince is awestruck, and I can't deny that I'm touched. "We made that."

I feel a momentary longing to have something more with him, which has happened on occasion since my conversation with Pearl. Like the night I asked Vince to stay for a movie.

I shake my head. No, we're going to be co-parents, that's all.

I wouldn't say I'm falling for Vince Fong, but I'm glad he's the one in this with me.

~

When Vince and I leave the clinic, we head to a nearby Indonesian restaurant that I quite like. We get a table and order satay, nasi goreng, semur daging, and urab. The latter is a vegetable dish with grated fresh coconut, and it's one of my favorites.

Our chicken satay with peanut sauce arrives, and I eagerly dig in. Though my stomach wasn't doing so hot earlier, I'm hungry now.

Yep, that "pregnant and hungry" shirt would definitely be appropriate, but I only wear it at home. I found it online several weeks ago and couldn't help myself from ordering it.

"By the way, I signed our baby up for daycare," I say.

"Already? You're planning on taking your full year of maternity leave, aren't you?"

"I am, but you have to get on the waiting lists early. People often sign up well before the baby arrives."

"Oh." He has a bite of chicken. "I was thinking I could be a stay-at-home dad, actually."

Although Vince said he wanted to be fairly involved, I never imagined him doing something like this.

"How would it work?" I ask tentatively. "Since we won't be living together."

"I'm still hoping you'll change your mind about that. But if not, I can come over to your place every morning and leave when you get home, if that's okay." He pauses. "Assuming you would like to keep your job. If you want to stay home for a few years, I can arrange for that, financially. I figured you'd want to work, though."

He's right. Maintaining financial independence is important to me, and taking myself out of the workforce for a few years and having a gap in my resume could make things more difficult.

But I like the idea of our child being cared for at home, or maybe going to daycare part-time. It never occurred to me as a possibility, though. I couldn't expect that much childcare of my mother, but if this is what Vince wants to do…

I just can't wrap my mind around it. This man is known for going to parties all the damn time. Women. Alcohol. Looking hot in suits.

But the picture of him chasing after a toddler is just as attractive.

Maybe this would make my ovaries twitch if I wasn't already, you know, pregnant.

The rest of our food arrives. The fried rice is a little greasy and delicious. The semur daging—a tender beef stew with sweet soy sauce and spices—is even better, and I moan in bliss. The urab is just as good as I remember and provides me with important vegetables.

I pop a green bean in my mouth and smile at Vince.

I haven't seen Carrie Lo since the night of the party. She wants to meet at one of our usual bars downtown, and I don't protest.

When she slides into the seat across from me, she asks, "What are you drinking?"

"Orange juice."

"Are you feeling okay?"

"Yeah, I'm fine. But I'm pregnant, so no alcohol for me."

"*You're pregnant?*" she screeches, and a few heads turn in our direction. "Sorry," she says, more quietly. "It just wasn't what I was expecting."

I chuckle. "Same here. Actually, I think I got pregnant the last night we saw each other."

"Did I look at you just right and"—she snaps her fingers—"your egg got fertilized?"

"Wouldn't that be something." I pause. "Or maybe I got pregnant the next day…or the day after that. But it was definitely that weekend. Since immaculate conception is unlikely, and that's the only weekend I had sex in the past year."

Carrie's mouth falls open as she makes the connection.

I'm kind of enjoying this.

My friend is wearing a silver dress with sequins that would look ridiculous on some people—like me—but on her, it's glamorous. Her black hair falls in soft waves.

But the expression on her face is anything but sophisticated.

"No way!" she says. "Vince Fong is the father?"

"Yep." And somehow, I can't help smiling as I say that.

She stands up and gives me a hug. "OMG, this is so exciting! Are *you* excited? How are you feeling?"

"I'm doing well now, actually."

"Vince knows you're pregnant?"

"Yeah. He's excited, too. I had my first ultrasound today, and he came."

"It's hard to imagine him as a father," Carrie says, "but I'm glad. Maybe this is why he's been acting weird."

"He has? You've seen him?"

"Nah, but you know my friend Pru? She was at Brian's party—although maybe that wasn't until after you left. But she said something off-hand about Vince acting odd lately. He actually turned her down when she propositioned him!" Carrie says this quietly, confidentially, as though it's the most shocking thing.

Vince said he'd be faithful to me, and I'm pleased he seems to be keeping his word.

It actually makes me a little giddy.

"Please don't tell anyone," I say. "Vince's family doesn't know yet, but he plans to tell them soon."

"Don't worry, your secret is safe with me. I mean, except for the fact that I yelled, 'You're pregnant?' when you told me. But now, my lips are sealed." Carrie mimes zipping her lips. "I am going to be the *coolest* auntie. None of my other friends have children yet, so I'll have lots of time for yours."

"You'll buy the most impractical baby clothes," I say. With affection.

"I will! Your baby is going to be so smart and good-looking, between you and Vince. You're not together now, are you? It's Vince Fong, so I wouldn't assume so, but he did turn down Pru..."

"He wants us to be a family. In fact, he asked me to marry him as soon as he found out I was pregnant."

"He did *what*?"

Man, I enjoy the way Carrie gets so excited. Her energy is infectious.

"He asked me to marry him," I repeat with a smile. "I said no, of course. I hardly know him. Well, I know him better now than I did back then. The offer's still on the table, and I'm not thinking of saying yes, not really, but..." I shrug. "Sometimes I think we could be together. Is that foolish of me?"

There. I admitted it.

"He *is* your baby daddy, and he's pretty hot."

"That's not enough, of course."

"No." She pauses. "I don't know him well, mostly just by reputation, but people do change. Maybe Vince could be a family man and a good husband."

"Whenever I'm craving something, he drops what he's doing and brings it to me." I tell her about what happened with the first cheesecake.

She doubles over in laughter. "He liiiiikes you."

"He's just being nice to the woman he knocked up."

"Marissa." She takes my hands in hers. "I'm sure it's more than that. You *broke* Vince Fong. In a good way. And I'm the one who introduced you two!"

"Umm, I don't think that's quite how it went. I thought he was hot, you told me who he was. That's basically it."

"Details, details."

I won't tell her that Vince cried at the ultrasound. It seems too personal.

"Ooh," Carrie says, "I found *the* perfect maternity dress."

"Already? You've known I was pregnant for all of ten minutes."

"My colleague, she's almost eight months pregnant, and she was wearing *such* a great outfit the other day. I made her show me where she got the dress. Just, you know, for future reference. You don't need it yet, but I'm going to get it for when you do."

I put up the obligatory protest, but I know Carrie will get it anyway.

"I don't know anything about babies," she says, "but I will watch YouTube videos—"

"I'm not sure YouTube is the best way to learn such things."

"—and then I can look after the baby for an afternoon so you can have some me-time. Maybe you'll just want to shower and nap. But Auntie Carrie will be there!"

I didn't cry at the ultrasound, but tears come to my eyes now as I think of the family and support network that me and the baby will have.

My mother didn't have that when I was little. I wish she had.

Carrie hands me some napkins and I dab my eyes. Then she comes around the table and gives me a long hug.

Which is exactly what I need.

When I get home on Friday, there's a package waiting for me at the front desk.

Inside the box is a burgundy maternity wrap dress, and I'm pleased it's suitable for the office. There's also a gift certificate for a mother-to-be session—whatever that entails—at a local spa, as well as some bling. But although Carrie favors showy pieces for herself, she's good at understanding other people's tastes. It's a simple heartbeat necklace, and considering I recently heard my baby's heartbeat for the first time, it seems particularly appropriate.

I'm about to text Carrie to thank her for the gift when I get a message from Vince. *Can I order you dinner tonight? I have something in mind.*

It's like he knew I wasn't in the mood to cook.

An hour later, I get a delivery from a Malaysian restaurant. There's lots of food, including roti canai with chicken curry.

Since it's more than enough for one person, I ask Vince if he wants to come over to help me with it, but he says he's busy and today is the day he's going to tell his family.

Oh. I can't help feeling nervous.

What if they don't react well to the news?

[15]

VINCE

"GUESS WHAT?" I say to Evie as I drive a firetruck over the play mat. "I'm going to tell the family my secret today. You remember what I told you before, don't you?"

I turn Evie in my lap so she's facing me, and she looks at me solemnly.

"You're getting a baby cousin, remember?"

Evie sticks her fingers in her mouth, which I'm sure is a sophisticated baby way of saying, *Yes, Uncle Vince, I remember everything.*

"I bet they'll be at least as cute as you. After all, I'm better-looking than your father."

She scrunches up her face and looks skeptical.

"No," I say, "I'm not sure whether it'll be a girl or a boy. Which would you prefer?"

"*You're having a baby?*"

I whip my head around. Courtney and Julian are standing at the door.

"Uh," I say. "I mean, I'm not pregnant, obviously. But a woman is having my baby, yes."

Geez, I'm usually a little smoother than this.

Courtney and Julian come into the room, their mouths hanging open. Eventually, Courtney kneels down beside me and gives me a hug.

"What's Uncle Vince been telling you?" She picks up Evie. "You've known for weeks, haven't you? And you didn't say anything?"

Evie gurgles.

"Are you happy?" Courtney asks me. "I assume it was unexpected."

"Yeah." I turn to my brother. "I wasn't stupid and careless. We took appropriate precautions, but you know, not everything is a hundred percent. But I'm happy."

Julian says nothing for a long time, but finally he cracks a smile. "You're definitely not better-looking than me."

I throw my head back and laugh, and then I swear them to secrecy.

My whole family is coming over to Julian and Courtney's house today, and it's the perfect time to say something. I would have told them last Sunday, but we went out to a Chinese restaurant in Scarborough for lunch, one of those crowded restaurants that white people don't go to—unless they're married to Asians—with brisk weekend service. It just wasn't the right time.

Tonight, however, is different.

I wait until we're eating dessert. Julian has baked lemon squares, and I pour myself another cup of jasmine tea before saying, "I have an announcement."

"You got a girl pregnant?" Cedric says. "I knew this would happen eventually."

I look at Courtney. "You told him?"

"Wasn't me," she says. "Evie must have done it."

Evie squawks from her high chair.

"Wait, are you serious?" Cedric asks. "I was just kidding! I thought you'd gotten a job or started a company."

I glare at him. "I'm serious. She's thirteen weeks along."

"Ah, this is exactly what I told you to do!" Po Po nods approvingly. "I said you were getting old, you should have a baby. Who is this woman? How long have you been together? When will you get married?"

"We're not a couple." I won't lie to my family. "But she's pregnant, and it's mine."

"I don't understand."

Mom hisses something to Po Po in Toisanese before turning to me. "We'll be thrilled to have another grandbaby, of course. I hope that, even though you aren't together, you will be an important part of the child's life and bring them to see us regularly."

"Of course."

"When I asked if you wanted to be a dad the other week," Cedric says, "did you already know?"

"Yeah. Marissa just didn't want me to tell anyone until she was out of the first trimester."

"This is not right," Po Po says. "I will go to your place and play Chinese opera music until you marry her."

"Look." I don't want to mention that Marissa turned me down and I'd still very much like to change her mind. "It's the twenty-first century and sometimes things happen differently now, but don't worry, the child will be well cared for."

Po Po clucks her tongue. "The parents should be together. I understand, sometimes you marry and it doesn't work out, so you divorce. But you should at least try to be married. I'm sure *Marissa* would appreciate it."

I shake my head. "It's not what she wants."

"I hope you will at least stop going to parties and playing videogames all the time. You must set a good example for your child."

"I will, don't worry." I pause. "Do you think I'll be a bad father?"

"Of course not," Mom says. "I will admit that, as your mother, some of the choices you make are not exactly what I want for you, but whenever you really want something, you succeed."

Julian doesn't say anything, but he nods once, and I smile. As much as I like bugging the shit out of him, his opinion does mean a lot to me.

"Tell us about Marissa," Courtney says.

"She's an engineer. Her family's from Hong Kong." I don't know how to describe Marissa. "She's a little bit bossy. In a good way."

Po Po cackles with glee.

"I want to meet her before the baby comes," Mom says. "Even if you're not together, she will be part of our family. You should bring her over sometime."

"Yes," Dad says. "Please do."

"We could throw her a baby shower?" Courtney suggests.

"She might have other people to do it, but I'll let her know you're willing."

"I guess this is exciting," Po Po says, "even if you are not getting married, like I want."

"When do I ever do what you tell me?"

"This is a good point. You are not very obedient. I bet your child will be the same. Will give you so much trouble!" My grandma seems delighted by this possibility.

"Yes," Dad says, eyes twinkling. "I hope he or she empties two whole bottles of shampoo on the living room carpet."

"And brings the hose and sprinkler inside the house to water the houseplants," Mom adds. "The couch got soaked."

"What about the poop explosion at his first birthday party?"

"Or the time he threw up on Julian at the grocery store?"

"I remember that," Julian says. "I also remember when he ate my entire birthday cake."

"That's right!" Mom says. "You wanted a *fancy* chocolate cake, so we got you one from the bakery. But we made the mistake of leaving it on the counter, and Vince climbed on a chair, sat on the cake, and ate it. He was so sick that night."

"Then there was General Bloopy the Bloopisauraus." Dad turns to Courtney. Everyone else already knows about General Bloopy. "A stuffed purple dinosaur he carried *everywhere* for two years."

"It was actually a brachiosaurus," Julian clarifies, "but he insisted it was a bloopisaurus, and every time, I would correct him."

"You were so annoying," I mutter.

"Unfortunately," Dad says, "General Bloopy got left out on the lawn one day, and when the kid across the street came over to mow the grass, he mowed right over General Bloopy."

Wait a second. I haven't heard this part of the story before.

"I told Vince that General Bloopy went to the spa for a week," Mom says, "because it was very important for dinosaur health. But really, I was running around to toy stores across the city, trying to find the exact stuffed dinosaur. When I finally did, I almost wept with joy."

My mind has been blown. I sit there slack-jawed.

"Oh, shit." Cedric laughs. "He didn't know."

"Uh, of course I knew," I say. "I figured it out. I was a smart kid."

"You sure ate a lot of Play-Doh for a smart kid."

"Remember when he ate the mushroom in the backyard?" Dad asks. "We had to call poison control."

"Alright, everyone." I hold up my hands. "I get it. I was a terror as a child—"

"Well, I'm not sure I'd go that far," Mom says.

"It could have been worse," Dad adds.

"—but I've heard enough stories for tonight," I say.

"He's struggling to get over the true story of General Bloopy." Julian smirks.

Dammit, it's my job to piss him off, not the other way around.

"Anyway," Mom says, "I'm sure your child will be a perfectly-behaved angel..." She can't finish her sentence. She's already cracking up with laughter.

You know, I'm looking forward to thirty years from now, when I'll be able to bug my own son or daughter about their childhood antics.

And I can't help hoping Marissa will be there beside me.

MY MORNING SICKNESS HAS IMPROVED, but I still have cravings that come out of nowhere.

Today, I have a new craving: Italian sausages and bakeapple jam.

I know, I know, it's a weird craving. They're not things I've ever had in combination.

Bakeapples aren't actually apples, but a kind of berry, also known as cloudberries. Pearl brought me some bakeapple jam after her trip to Newfoundland, and I really loved it. When I finished the jar, I found a specialty food store in Toronto where I could purchase it, and I pick some up about once a year.

I don't have any at home right now, however.

And that specialty food store just so happens to be downtown, maybe a fifteen-minute walk from where Vince lives.

Funny coincidence, isn't it?

It's a Sunday morning, so I'm home. I text him, asking if he'll get sausages and bakeapple jam for me.

Not even a minute later, he replies, saying he'll be over in an hour.

I'm excited.

Mostly because I'll be eating bakeapple jam and sausages.

And a little—okay, more than a little—because I'll be seeing Vince.

When he arrives, he's loaded down with food. He's wearing jeans and a Henley again, and I wonder how many people get to see this version of Vince Fong, the dressed-down version who runs around town buying food for someone else.

I kiss him. I can't help it.

"Hey, Marissa," he murmurs. "You see something you like?"

"Yeah. Lots and lots of food. You got the things I wanted?"

"I most certainly did." He carries the bags of food into the kitchen, where he pulls out a package of uncooked mild Italian sausages and a jar of bakeapple jam. "I'll get these sausages cooking for you right away."

Normally I wouldn't let someone else cook in my kitchen, but I'm not going to stop Vince from cooking for me.

I remove the rest of the items from the bags. There's a baguette and a box of fancy crackers. A ready-made green salad. A fruit salad. Two types of cheese—but not the kinds I can't eat. A large piece of chocolate cake.

"Is that enough for both of us?" He looks over his shoulder and winks at me.

"Yeah, I think so." I'm already opening up the cheese. I put some on a slice of baguette and top it with bakeapple jam. "Mmm, that's good."

"I've never had bakeapple before."

I spread some jam on a small cracker, walk over to the stove, and hold the cracker up to his lips. He eats the food from my hands.

I'm about to ask what he thought when he says, "Did you just drool on the sausages?"

Damn, I was hoping he wouldn't notice.

"Uh, yeah."

"Is that because I'm irresistible?"

I roll my eyes. "You're very resistible."

"Sure. That's why you're pregnant with my baby."

The way he casually says it...something sizzles, and it's not the sausages in the pan. The fabric of my "pregnant and hungry" shirt feels uncomfortable. I want out of these clothes.

I also really want those sausages. They're the reason I drooled.

No really, they are.

But I'm turned on, too. A man looking after me is pretty sexy. It's been a while since I've had a boyfriend, someone who'd prepare food for me like this.

Not, of course, that Vince is my boyfriend.

He just knocked me up.

Oh, God. Why do I want to press myself against him and hump his leg?

No, self. You are not having sex with Vince. Too complicated right now.

He is, however, more like the men I date than I initially thought, aside from his wealth and ridiculous good looks.

"Are those sausages done yet?" I ask as I take out the butter. It's a bit hard, but I do my best to spread it on a slice of baguette.

Hard.

I need to remove such words from my vocabulary.

I cut several slices of cheese and baguette, then put two plates on the table. I fill my plate with salad.

Just kidding. I help myself to a little of both salads before placing a generous amount of cheese, bread, and crackers on my plate, just as Vince comes over with the sausages.

Sausages. Hard.

I'm practically shaking with excitement, and I'm definitely drooling.

And now I'm embarrassed that I'm wearing a large—though appropriate—"pregnant and hungry" shirt and literally drooling over sausages.

Perhaps I should have dressed up for his visit. Like, put on clothes that aren't pajamas.

Vince deposits two sausages on each plate before helping himself to some salad. For a few minutes, we eat in silence, me wolfing down my food at an alarming rate, him eating at a more sensible pace.

It feels very domestic, just sharing a meal together at my condo.

"So, you told your family about the pregnancy? How did it go?"

I may have spoken while chewing. I just can't help stuffing my face with all this delicious food.

"It went fine."

That's a slightly terse response, coming from Vince Fong.

"It doesn't sound like it went fine," I say, my heart hammering.

He takes in my expression. "I didn't mean to worry you. They're happy. Surprised, of course, but happy. My grandma isn't thrilled that we're not married, but she'll get over it. She was pleased when I called you bossy."

"Hey! I am *not* bossy."

Vince looks pointedly at the food on the table.

"I'm not bossy," I say. "I'm pregnant. And you told me to text you whenever I needed anything, and I *needed* these sausages."

To emphasize my point, I pop a bite of sausage and bakeapple jam in my mouth, and this time, I don't hold back my groan of pleasure. In fact, I make the groan just a little obscene.

Vince's eyes are heavy-lidded.

I wipe my mouth with a napkin. "Yes, that was definitely necessary sausage."

"I believe you."

"Don't use that sarcastic tone on me!"

His lips twitch. "I'm not trying to sound sarcastic. I do believe you. And I've never been pregnant, so who am I to argue? Most of the time I've known you, you've been growing another person inside you, so I'm not well acquainted with what you're like otherwise."

"Aside from that weekend."

"*That* weekend. Yes."

Although I made orgasmic sounds a few minutes ago, his smoldering gaze still surprises me. I feel bloated and clumsy and I'm hardly dressed for company.

Yet he looks at me just like he did on the night we met.

"Anyway," he says, "getting back to my family dinner... They, uh, started teasing me about all the things I did in my childhood. Like eating Play-Doh and pouring shampoo on the carpet. Stuff like that."

Ah. I smile. "Those don't sound so bad. What else did you do?"

He scratches the back of his neck. "I had a stuffed dinosaur called General Bloopy the Bloopisaurus that I carried everywhere. Apparently he was destroyed and replaced at one point, and my mom lied to me and said he went to a spa."

"Oh, the outrage!" I laugh.

"The point," Vince says, leaning forward, "is that they all seem convinced our child will be a terror. I apologize in advance."

I'm not fazed by this. Children are always a bit troublesome. I doubt ours will be a complete terror.

And that dinosaur story? It's cute.

"Who was at your family dinner on Friday?" I ask.

"My mom, my dad, my grandma. My oldest brother, Julian, and his wife and baby. My other brother Cedric."

"That sounds nice." I have a bite of salad. "I know my mom wanted to have more kids, but..." I pause. "My dad died when I was three, a few months after we came to Canada. He was hit by a car. My mom asked him to go to the convenience store for a bag of Cheetos, and he never came back."

"Marissa," he says, reaching across the table. He brushes his fingers against mine, and I grab onto him. "I'm so sorry."

"I want our child to have what I didn't. Extended family

nearby. Another parent. That's why it's so important to me that you be involved."

"Thank you for telling me." He squeezes my hand. "I will do the best I can, I promise."

I swallow, my throat a bit scratchy.

"Anyway," I say, sounding more upbeat than I feel, "my dad's death cast a cloud over my childhood, and my mother had to work hard to provide for us. I couldn't cause trouble for her. Not that she was overly strict, but she was always tired, always working."

I look at the last bite of sausage on my plate. I'm not craving it anymore.

"You going to eat that?" Vince asks.

"Nah, you can have it."

He finishes the sausage, then takes out the plastic container with chocolate cake.

Yes, that's exactly what I need. My mouth starts watering again. He slides his chair around the table so we're sitting next to each other, and he lifts a forkful of chocolate cake to my mouth.

I moan. "Oh, that's delicious."

He has a bite of his own. "It is, isn't it?" He pats himself on the back. "Good job, Vince."

I roll my eyes, but my heart feels full. Vince has been here for me, he's listened, and that's just what I needed.

From lusting after him while he cooked sausages…to this.

It's a little overwhelming.

After we finish the cake—Vince lets me eat two-thirds of it— he takes my hand and leads me to the couch in the living room. He pulls me into his lap, and for a while, we just sit there together.

Eventually, he cups the back of my head and brings my mouth down to his.

He kisses me slowly, gently, as though we have more than a night or a weekend. I feel both boneless and a little keyed-up.

"Can I ask you something?" he says.

I nod, even though I have no idea what he's going to say, and it makes me a bit nervous.

"Will you go on a date with me?"

"You asked me to marry you when I told you I was pregnant. Now you just want a date?"

"Well, you weren't happy with the proposal. You—quite reasonably—pointed out that we hardly knew each other, so let's spend more time together. A date."

I hesitate. "Why haven't you had a girlfriend since university?"

"For many years, I had no time. My company was my life."

"Which was your choice."

"True. I'm not good at balance, which is why I burnt out. Badly."

Sometimes it's hard for me to picture Vince's former life, given his playboy image. But I can see it now, can imagine his utter devotion to his work.

I can imagine him burning out, too, and there's an ache in my chest.

"Then I sold it," he says, "and I was suddenly free. But at that point, it didn't feel like a choice. I had to change. I just couldn't continue."

"So that's when you went all-out on with your life of leisure."

"Life of leisure. Yeah." He pauses. "A relationship didn't appeal to me. Too much commitment. But also…the past few years have been a mess of burn-out and depression. I wasn't in a good place."

I squeeze his hand.

"Now," he says, "I'm doing better and I do want the commitment. I want you and our baby together. That's what matters to me now."

"You can be a dedicated father without being with the mother of your child."

"Yes, but I want you, too. I told you that I could just give you a weekend, but it was the best weekend of my life, truly."

"Mm-hmm. That's why you made no effort to contact me."

"It's what I know," he says apologetically, "but I'm trying, Marissa. I want to kiss you when we wake up in the middle of the night to the baby's cries. I want to get matcha double fromage cheesecake for you even when you don't have pregnancy cravings. Let's go on a date and see how it goes, okay?"

"Okay," I whisper. "Next Friday?"

"I'll pick you up at seven."

He kisses me, and I lean against him.

I'm tired. Maybe from everything we've just said to each other about his burn-out, and my dad, and General Bloopy. I'm probably also going into some kind of food coma after all the sausages, bakeapple jam, cheese, and chocolate cake.

Vince does indeed treat me well, and I feel like I understand him better now.

I don't love him. I'm not ready to marry him.

But I've started to feel open to the idea of a relationship. I don't think it would be a good idea to jump into bed together just yet, though.

Bed. Mmm. What a lovely thought.

As if reading my mind—or maybe just noticing that my eyelids are closing—Vince gathers me in his arms and carries me into the bedroom.

I do want to sleep, but first…

I pick up a faded photo from my night table. The photo that has been resting on my night table for as long as I remember, in all the different places I've lived.

"That's my dad," I say.

It was the eighties, and he's wearing glasses that seem woefully uncool now. Or maybe they've become cool again—I'm not an expert on these things. Carrie would know.

My dad is holding me. I'm in a fussy pink dress, grinning impishly at the camera, and my dad sports a similar grin.

He's looking at me as though I'm the greatest thing that ever happened to him.

At least, that's what I always imagined when I looked at this picture.

My mom told me real stories about him, but sometimes she'd invent fantastical stories in which he'd save the day. I'd listen with rapt attention, and I did my best to behave.

But one time when I was thirteen, I wanted to go to the mall with my friends, and my mom wouldn't let me because I had chores and schoolwork.

"I bet Dad would have let me," I shot back.

As soon as I said it, I knew I'd gone too far.

My normally-stoic mother burst into tears.

The absence of my father has been a part of my life for as long as I can remember, but this pregnancy has made it more difficult than it's been in years. The major life change…it makes me think of what might have been.

Pearl's pregnancies were planned, unlike mine, and she put off having children for a while because she couldn't imagine doing it without her mother, who'd died when Pearl was twenty-three. She couldn't imagine not having her mother to turn to for help— and to provide unwanted advice. She couldn't imagine being in the hospital with her new baby and not getting a visit from her mom, who'd coo over the baby and say they were beautiful no matter what.

And then you add shit like this on top of pregnancy hormones and complicated feelings for the father of your baby, who opened up to me in a way I suspect he rarely does.

When I met him, I saw only one thing.

But I've begun to trust him. Trust him with more than my pleasure, which I'm actually *not* trusting him with right now, in part because I'm afraid it would mean something, unlike that first weekend, and I'm not ready for that yet. It's hard for me to have meaningless sex with a guy when I'm having his baby.

Though I did agree to the date.

Vince kisses me again, and I feel raw and vulnerable and safe all at the same time. I didn't tell him everything going through my mind, but somehow, I feel like he knew.

When I wake up from my nap two hours later, Vince is gone. He's left a small slice of chocolate cake—where did it come from? I thought we ate all the cake?—on a plate with fruit salad, next to a fork on the kitchen table. There's also a "pregnant and cute" shirt, which makes me chuckle.

I send him a text.

Thank you.

[17]

VINCE

I SET out to prove to Marissa that I'm more than a playboy. That was my goal. Then she'd hopefully fall in love with me and agree to marry me, and I would have the family life that I suddenly craved.

I would devote myself to being a good father and husband.

But whenever I do something for Marissa, it's not because of my goal. I don't think to myself, *This will make her like me more!*

I do things for her because it's what I want to do.

I like seeing her drool while I cook sausages. I love the way she moans when she eats cheesecake. I love telling her stories about my family and childhood so she can gently laugh at me.

I enjoy these quiet moments.

It didn't used to be this way. I used to need everything to be as loud and hedonistic as possible, as I tried to forget about my inner turmoil. Even when that life started to lose its appeal, I didn't know what else to do with myself.

But then there was Evie. She'd wrap her tiny hand around my finger and give me a glimmer of a smile, and that filled me with joy.

And then there was Marissa and our unborn child.

I wanted her to fall in love with me because she said love was a requirement for marriage for her. I figured I'd come to love her, but I didn't think about my feelings too much; I was focused on Marissa.

And now, it's happened.

I've fallen in love.

I can't pinpoint exactly when it happened, but sometime between the appointments and running around to get her food and kissing her in her kitchen and bantering and listening and tucking her into bed...

Yes, I'm in love now, and I'm determined that our first date—weird to think of a first date when she's pregnant with my child—will be wonderful.

It can't be too showy though, because Marissa wouldn't like that.

She can't drink alcohol or eat raw fish...and various other things, so there are some limitations. I also don't want to go to any of my usual haunts, because I don't want anyone to recognize me. I don't think Marissa would enjoy that.

Well, this will be a bit of a challenge, but I'm up for it.

Friday night finally arrives.

I doubt Marissa wants to be shuttled around by a driver, so I drive myself. I park in the outside visitors' parking area at her condo and take the elevator up to the third floor, as I've done several times before.

When she opens the door, I grin. She's wearing a red dress that doesn't show a huge amount of skin, but it clings to her curves. Curves I haven't gotten a close look at since January.

But I remember every detail.

Her body looks a little different now, thanks to the pregnancy, and I feel a possibly-ridiculous sense of pride.

"Shit."

That's the first word she says to me.

"Are we going somewhere really fancy?" she asks, taking in my outfit. "I'm not dressed for that."

"You look lovely," I say, "but if you don't feel like being seen with me in a three-piece suit, perhaps I can take you to the bedroom instead?" I lean casually against the doorframe.

She rolls her eyes.

I don't know why, but I enjoy her eye rolls.

"No, we're going out," she says. "I can get changed if I need to."

"You look perfect. Honestly, we're not going anywhere fancy. I just enjoyed the way you threw yourself at me the last time I wore this."

"I did not *throw* myself at you."

I smirk at her expression of outrage. "Fine, fine, you didn't *throw* yourself at me. You just said, and I quote, 'You're really fucking handsome in that suit,' and kissed me. Now, I have lots of plans for tonight. Let's head out."

We go downstairs and I help her into my car. I haven't seen her in almost a week, not since I realized I love her, and it feels like far too long. I itch to touch her more, but I'll save that for later.

It takes us close to half an hour to get to our destination. I park on the street and lead her to a bar on Ossington.

She looks at me skeptically. "Is the food really good?"

"No, we're eating somewhere else."

"You know I can't drink."

"Yes, I'm aware."

She doesn't ask any further questions as we head inside. I've gotten to know this bar well over the past week. It's one of these quirky, dimly-lit places with antique lampshades. I lead her to the back corner, where there are two red armchairs by a low wood table. There's a menu on the table, and I hand it to Marissa.

"There's an extensive selection of mocktails on the last page," I say. "So I can still take you out for drinks even though you can't have alcohol."

I hope she likes this. I spent a lot of time looking online for mocktails in the city, and then I went out and tried three places. This one was the best. I came back a second time so I could try more drinks, the better to properly advise Marissa.

"The one with ginger beer is my favorite," I say. "Ginger beer, pear, and vanilla. It works really well."

Ugh, maybe I'm trying too hard. I don't know. "Trying too hard" hasn't been a problem for me in the past few years, but yeah, I did extensive research on mocktails just for this date.

"You come here regularly?" Marissa asks. "And you're familiar with the mocktails? I'd expect you to drink, well, alcohol."

"I knew nothing about mocktails until five days ago."

And then I went totally overboard.

Her eyes soften.

"Vince," she says, patting my hand.

Nobody looks at me like Marissa does. Nobody else is moved by my actions.

Will she come to love me?

I swallow. "Anyway, if that ginger beer mocktail sounds good to you, you should get it."

"Okay," she says, but rather than putting down the menu, she continues to study it. "I'm curious about the one with lemon, rosemary simple syrup, and muddled strawberries."

"I haven't tried it before," I say. "I'll get it and you can have a taste, alright?"

She nods before turning back to the menu, as though she cannot leave a single menu item unstudied, even if she knows what she's ordering. She's thorough. I like it.

I wonder if she'll read several baby name books cover to cover.

"I'd like to get some food, too," she says.

"You're worried you won't get enough to eat later? Trust me, there's no need to worry. I'm taking you to a restaurant with large servings."

"Ooh, where are we going?"

"It's a secret."

"I don't like secrets."

"Somehow this doesn't surprise me, but I'm keeping it a secret."

It looks like she's trying to shoot daggers at me with her eyes, but fortunately, she fails.

Though she does succeed in looking sexy.

"I'm still going to order food," she says. "Those lemon-rosemary savory donuts sound amazing, and I think they'll perfectly complement your drink."

She makes a compelling argument. When the waitress comes around, we order drinks as well as donuts. I don't miss the appreciative glance that the waitress gives me, and when she walks away, Marissa makes another attempt to shoot daggers, this time at the back of the waitress's head.

A woman acting possessive. I never expected to enjoy it so much.

"So, why engineering?" I ask. "Why did you decide to study it?"

She seems momentarily disoriented, then says, "I was good at math and physics. I wanted a degree that was geared toward a career without spending ten years in school. The job market was a little rough when I graduated, but I found something eventually."

"It's not a deep passion?

She shakes her head. "I like it and it suits me, but I don't love it. I'm okay with that. My passion is having a steady, secure, balanced life, in which I don't have to overwork myself to pay the bills, or feel guilty when I get a latte instead of a drip coffee."

I find that fascinating. I guess I took some of those things for granted—security and not worrying about how I'd pay the bills.

Steady and balanced? Not so much.

Growing up, I knew many people whose families were all about more, more, *more*. There could always be more money, more prestige, and often it came at the expense of other things.

Me? I throw myself headlong into a project and think about nothing else. I couldn't tell I was burnt out until I was barely able to function.

In the past few years, I relished cultivating as ridiculous of an image as possible. I played it up with my family, too. The outrageous youngest son.

But in part thanks to Courtney, I've gotten a little better at considering my mental health and having some balance in my life, even if "balance" isn't sexy.

And I don't think Marissa is ordinary or boring for how she lives her life.

I think she's amazing.

The waitress brings over our mocktails. Marissa wraps her lips around her straw and sips her drink. "It's delicious."

I try mine. It's pretty good, but not as good as the ginger beer mocktail.

"Let me try yours." She reaches for my drink as soon as I put it down, and I can't help a chuckle. "Mmm, that's even better."

"Then we can switch, since I prefer the ginger beer one."

Funny how that worked out.

Our donuts arrive five minutes later. There are four on the plate, plus a little dish of aioli. Marissa breaks one in half and dunks it in the aioli.

"Good?" I ask.

"Yeah. Though it doesn't taste like a donut to me. More like a biscuit in a donut shape, not that I'm complaining. I can totally imagine myself getting cravings for these." She takes another bite. "Mocktails and savory donuts aren't what I expected tonight."

"What did you expect?" I stretch out on the chair, crossing one leg over the other.

"Oh, I don't know. Eating flambéed duck on a private boat or something like that."

"I did consider it," I say, stroking my chin. "Glad I opted for this place instead."

A few minutes later, a young man and woman walk past our table. Well, the man passes our table; the woman is distracted by our donuts.

"Those smell *so* good," she says. "I've been craving them all week." She pats her stomach—she's quite pregnant.

"I'm pregnant too!" Marissa says. "And I was *just* thinking that I might start craving them."

They laugh together and discuss their due dates, and when the other woman says, "I'll let you get back to your husband," Marissa doesn't protest her choice of words.

We stay for one more non-alcoholic drink, and then I drive to Roncesvalles for the next part of our date. We enter a Polish restaurant, a solid family place that has been around for a long time. It's almost eight o'clock now, and there are fewer families and more couples than when I went here earlier in the week.

I suggest we get the platter for two, which has pierogis, cabbage rolls, schnitzel, goulash, potato pancakes, and other things. Marissa nods briskly as she practically drools on the menu.

"You must think I'm absolutely obsessed with food," she says. "I promise, I'm not usually like this. Not to this extent, anyway."

"I don't mind."

She does indeed enjoy dinner—especially the potato pancakes —and by some miracle, we finish everything on the large platter.

The only issue comes at the end of the meal, when she tries to pay the bill and we spend ten minutes arguing about it.

Eventually, I let her pay so we don't stay here all night.

"What else do you have planned?" she asks as we waddle out of the restaurant. "I'm not sure I can eat more, and it's been ages since I felt this way."

"Well, we don't have to go, but there's an ice cream place nearby…"

"You're killing me." She laughs. She's laughed a lot tonight, and it makes me smile every time. "Alright, let's go. We might have to share something. Not sure I could have my own."

We end up splitting a raspberry-balsamic sorbet, and Marissa keeps swirling her tongue over her spoon and generally driving me mad.

And she knows *exactly* what she's doing.

The drive back is mostly silent, but I'm very aware of her sitting next to me, wearing that clingy red dress. When we get to her building, I help her out of the car, then immediately drop my mouth to her lips and slide my leg between hers. When I stroke my tongue into her mouth, she presses herself against my leg and circles her hips.

My mind travels back to that weekend. I lifted her up and fucked her against my door. I remember how it felt to have her gripping me, and I groan.

I want to slide inside her, and it has to be *her*, nobody else.

"Why were you at Brian's party?" I suddenly ask.

I'd never seen her at one of his parties before, and I know it sounds silly, but now it feels like fate that she was there.

"I'm friends with Carrie Lo."

"She seems different from the kind of friends I imagine you having."

"We met at a bachelorette party a while back—she was the groom's sister—and we got along well. She started inviting me to things every now and then, and I liked hanging out with her. She prioritizes taking care of herself and doing things that make her feel good. She doesn't think of herself last, the way women are so often expected to do. When I told her I was pregnant, a flattering maternity dress and a gift certificate to a spa showed up that week. Things for me, not for the baby."

I wish I'd been the one to think of the spa thing.

I brush my fingers over her collarbone. "I'm glad you were there that night."

"If I'm honest, I really wanted to let loose after my mom's health scare."

I stiffen. Marissa grew up without much family. Her mom is very important to her.

"She's fine," Marissa says hurriedly. "I'd just gotten the good news. I was relieved and feeling indulgent, and Carrie told me about a party. You know the rest."

"No, I don't believe I do. Tell me."

"Dammit, Vince."

Before she can fling any more swear words at me, I kiss her again. I slip my hand under the neckline of her dress and fondle her breast. Her nipple pebbles under my touch.

"Indulge yourself again tonight," I murmur. "Let's take this upstairs."

I push myself against her and show her exactly how ready I am.

When she sighs—and not with pleasure—I immediately step back.

"I can't," she says.

"It wouldn't hurt the baby. I've done research."

Her eyes flicker with amusement. I can see it, even in the poor lighting. I've become accustomed to looking for every nuance in her expression. Actually I don't have to *look*; I just notice. I'm attuned to every little change in her.

"Last time..." She looks down. "We told ourselves—and each other—that it didn't mean anything. That it was just one weekend. But I won't lie. It can't be that simple now, and I'm not ready."

It's been too long and my body is on fire, but I know what she's saying. I won't push, even though I *am* ready.

I agree; it would be different this time. We know each other now. Okay, a lot of our interactions have been food-based, but still. We've exposed ourselves in ways that have nothing to do with bare skin.

Tonight, though, was a straightforward first date in many ways, but it's impossible to ignore everything that came before.

"Can I take you out again?" I ask, trying not to let fear creep into my voice.

That's what I really couldn't stand—if she wasn't willing to give me a chance to be more than the father of her child.

It terrifies me.

Not that I'll tell anyone, but I can admit it to myself.

I need her. Not simply to fulfill the cute domestic fantasy in my head, the fantasy that will make me feel like my life has meaning, but because she's Marissa, and she's lovely, even when she's scarfing down cabbage rolls like it's the end of the world.

I need her to return my feelings, and there are signs she might be heading in that direction, but what if I'm wrong? I don't know much about these things and—

"Yes," she says. "We can do that again."

Once I'm back in my car, pulling away from her building, I pump my fist in victory.

Why the hell are you happy? my dick asks. *I'm in pain!*

"Oh, shut up," I say.

Now I'm really losing it, because I'm talking out loud to my dick.

And yet all seems right with the world.

[18]
VINCE

THE MORNING after my first real date with Marissa, I'm frustrated with myself.

I didn't have a great sleep last night. I was rolling around in bed, wishing she was there with me. Wishing she'd wake up in the middle of the night and cuddle up to me, then wrap her lips around my cock and let me spend in her mouth.

I jerked myself off to the thought of her.

And now it's ten in the morning…and here I am again. In the shower this time, the water washing over my skin, my dick in my hand. I close my eyes and tip my head back as I remember the way she bit into that savory donut. The way she licked her lips after eating raspberry-balsamic sorbet.

If I have these foods again, I'll inevitably think of her.

I pump myself faster, wishing I was inside her instead of alone. I wouldn't have sex with her in the shower—I'm too worried about her slipping—but we could shower together, and afterward, I could dry her off with a towel and sit her on the counter…and then I could slide into her. Heaven. She'd wrap her legs around me and urge me on, making noises at least as erotic as the ones she makes when eating cheesecake.

I explode in my hand, then brace myself against the wall.

Now that my head isn't completely lost in thoughts of Marissa, I dimly recall that my dad plans to visit me this morning.

And I just jerked myself off in the shower. Lovely.

My dad rarely visits me by himself. Usually, my mother is with him.

I can't help worrying. What does he want to talk to me about alone?

Once I get out of the shower and put on semi-respectable clothes, it's ten thirty-five and my dad was supposed to arrive at ten thirty.

Dad, like Julian, is usually punctual. But a couple years ago, he arrived right on time at my penthouse…and let's just say, he saw some stuff that we both wish he hadn't seen. Ever since, he's made a point of coming exactly fifteen minutes late when he's meeting me at home.

Sure enough, he arrives at ten forty-five. I usher him inside and offer him tea, but he refuses.

We sit on couches in the living room, and when he doesn't immediately say anything, I glance out the window. One thing I love about this place is the view of the lake to the south. Every day, the sky and lake are slightly different colors. I'd never realized the lake could be so many different colors until I moved here.

I turn back to my dad. "So, what did I do this time?" I ask with a lopsided smile.

He's still quiet.

This is alarming.

"It's about Marissa," he says at last.

I grip the sofa. "What happened?"

"Nothing. I'm just a little worried… Vince, you're wealthy, and that's no secret. There are some people who might take advantage of you."

I lean forward. "What are you saying?"

"You're not stupid, even if you act like it sometimes."

"Thank you?"

"I'm sure you were using birth control, but do you think it's possible she tampered with it? She could be looking for a big child support payment. And are you certain the child is yours?"

Okay, now I'm seeing red.

"Dad, this is absurd."

"But there are people who will do such things."

"Not Marissa."

"How well do you know her?"

"Reasonably well."

"I know you're excited about being a father. I just want you to be aware of the possibility. I got to where I did in business because I didn't let people take advantage of me."

"Marissa would never do that," I say. "We haven't talked directly about support payments, but I offered to help her financially so she could stay home with the child until they start school, and she said no. It's important to her to be financially independent. She grew up without much money."

"So perhaps she wants the security of having yours."

"I offered to marry her, and she said no. Hell, I tried to pay for dinner last night, and after a ten-minute argument, I gave up and let her pay."

"I thought you two weren't together?"

"We're dating now."

"When you proposed to her, did you mean it?"

"Of course! Why else would I have done it? What do you take me for?"

But perhaps I shouldn't blame him. I've always been the not-so-serious, troublesome youngest child. Even when I was working 24/7, I acted that way with my family.

He frowns. "You love her?"

"I'm not answering that question."

I want Marissa to be the first person to know how I feel, not my dad when he's questioning her integrity.

"Has there been a paternity test?"

"You can do those before the baby is born?"

"There are ways, yes."

"I don't need a test to know the baby's mine."

There's no doubt in my voice. I know, in my bones, that she's not lying. She might tell little lies, like saying she only finds me a tiny bit attractive, but she would never have tampered with the condoms or tried to make me support a baby that isn't mine. She said there's no one else who could be the father, and I believe her.

The fact that my dad could think that of her…it makes me feel gross.

"You should leave," I say.

He nods. His calmness infuriates me

I follow him to the door.

"I'm just looking out for you," he says.

I sigh, a bit deflated. "I know."

And with that, he's gone.

That afternoon, I head to Brian's, and we relax in the glassed-in room at the back of his mansion with some fine merlot. I'm not in a great mood after my dad's visit—though the wine running through my veins does make me feel a touch better—and Brian picks up on it.

"You're still not yourself," he says. "Can you tell me what's up yet?"

I take a deep breath. "I'm going to be a father."

The look of horror on Brian's face is amusing.

I'm pretty sure it's not the idea of *me* being a father. Brian absolutely does not want to be a parent himself, as he's told me before, and he had a vasectomy last year. This would be his worst nightmare.

"Who's the mother?" he asks.

"The woman I met at your party in January."

"Which party?"

It's true. Brian had multiple parties in January.

"Her name's Marissa," I say. "She's Carrie's friend."

"That explains the cryptic comment Carrie made the other day." He sips his wine. "Though I'm still not sure why you've been weird and broody, uninterested in sleeping with women and..." He drops his voice, as though he's about to say something truly shocking. "Leaving parties before midnight."

I smirk, but then I say, "Brian, I'm going to be a dad. It changes things."

"It doesn't have to change much. Or are you worried about this happening again? You can get snipped."

"Nah."

"It doesn't make you any less of a man."

Anyone who thinks that is an idiot.

No, the thing is... I might want to have more kids?

Though I should probably wait to see how the first kid goes before I consider it.

It also requires Marissa to actually want to be with me. I doubt she'd want to make a second baby together otherwise.

Two sounds like enough, though.

"I'm not going to be the kind of dad who sees his child a few times a month," I say. "I want to be there for much more than that. I'm not going to keep partying all the time."

"Don't let this turn you into someone you're not."

"I know what I want."

Brian doesn't offer another protest. He simply nods. "You do what you gotta do." He slaps me on the shoulder. "Don't become a stranger."

"I won't, though I expect you'll see less of me."

He sighs. "Yeah, I know."

"I'm also dating Marissa. You know, the mother of my child."

"You're in a relationship?" He draws his eyebrows together, as though confused. As though this is beyond his comprehension.

"Not officially, but I promised to be exclusive."

Brian presses his palm to his mouth, like he's trying to stop wine from spewing out of it and onto his expensive carpet. Or expensive couch. Or expensive table.

"Exclusive?" he says. "You know what that word means, don't you?"

"Uh, yeah. Actually, I haven't had sex with anyone since that weekend in January."

He sputters. "You haven't…had sex…since January?"

"No."

I'm not happy about this situation, but still, I smile. I can't help being amused by Brian's reaction.

"When's the last time you went that long without getting laid?" he asks.

"Over a decade ago."

Even when I was spending most of my time on work, I'd still let loose once every month or two, and usually it involved sex.

Yep, a drought this long is unusual for me.

Yet I'm confident in my decision. There is no woman for me but Marissa, and she's not ready to sleep with me, therefore I'm not having sex.

"This is ridiculous." Brian shakes his head as he has a sip of wine.

"What's ridiculous?" Holden asks, entering the room.

"Hey, Holden," I say. "I didn't realize you were coming to Toronto this weekend."

He helps himself to some wine and leans back in a chair. "Tell me. What's ridiculous?"

"Vince hasn't had sex since January," Brian says.

"He's pulling your leg. Not possible."

"No, really," I say. "I got a woman pregnant, we're seeing each other, and I'm not sleeping with anyone else."

"But you're sleeping with her, at least."

"Not yet. Not since the weekend I met her."

Holden's eyes are wide and he's disturbingly still.

I think I've sent him into a state of shock. Crap, am I going to have to perform CPR?

Is it weird that this is more shocking to him than if I'd gone to Singapore last weekend, fucked a couple supermodels, gotten high on mushrooms, and accidentally stabbed my dick with a durian?

Man, I think I'm losing my touch when it comes to making up stories.

Finally, Holden starts breathing.

"Okay, here's the important question," he says. "Are you in love with her?"

"Yes."

Holden extends his hand to Brian and wiggles his fingers. "You owe me."

Brian sighs. "I do."

"What is going on?" I ask.

"We made a bet," Holden says. "When you were acting weird the last time I was here, I said you were in love. Brian thought I was wrong. And now, you've proven me correct."

I don't mention that I wasn't in love back then. "How much was the bet for?"

"A thousand bucks."

I'm weary of this useless life the three of us lead, where thousand-dollar bets are pocket change.

In fact, I'm disgusted with myself.

God, I *need* this kid. To have a family with Marissa. Not that I believe everyone needs to have kids, but I think this will give *my* life some value.

At the same time, I'm disgusted with myself for getting annoyed about this bet. I feel like I'm turning into Julian and have no sense of humor.

"He's mooning over her," Holden says to Brian.

"Never thought I'd see the day," Brian says.

"How long do you think this will last?"

"It will last," I growl.

"But you're Vince Fong," Holden says, and I wish I could change my name. "Three-night stands are too much commitment for you."

"Well, I've changed."

My friends look skeptical, probably assuming I'll be over Marissa in a few months and back to my usual ways.

I have news for them. I'm serious about her and our family.

But maybe they have a point.

What do I know about this sort of thing? I haven't had a relationship in ages. What do I even know about meaningful friendships? These guys are my closest friends, and they're not bad people, though they mostly care about having fun.

I don't doubt my current feelings for Marissa, but maybe it won't last. Yes, she's a great woman, but maybe I feel this way mainly because she's having my baby.

No, it's more than that. It's got to be.

Still, I can't say that with absolute certainty.

Dammit.

I gulp more wine and pour myself another glass. That's what Vince Fong does.

Yet last night, I was happily drinking mocktails.

I don't dare tell my friends about all the planning I did for that date. I don't tell them how I've been running around town, buying her every food she craves. I don't tell them that I cried at the ultrasound.

I don't tell them that I fear I'm unlovable, that in some ways, my cockiness is an act.

"I saw your brother the other day," Brian says.

"Julian?"

"No. Cedric. At least, I think it was him. At a café downtown. He's cute. I couldn't tell from the author picture on the back of his book, but he is."

"Don't you dare." It would be too weird, and I'm pretty sure Cedric isn't into casual sex like Brian is. I'm not even sure if my brother has any interest in men, but I have reason to think he might.

Or maybe Brian doesn't find Cedric attractive. Maybe he's just saying this to piss me off because he's annoyed that I'm not willing to join him in all his exploits anymore.

I finish my wine. "I should go."

"Vince!" Brian calls after me as I hurry toward his front door, but I don't reply.

I spend Saturday night alone, something I never, ever do.

[19]

MARISSA

I have a problem.

I'd heard that some women get super horny during pregnancy, particularly in their second trimester—even my own mother told me this—but I thought it wouldn't happen to me.

Yet here I am.

I've already masturbated twice today to take the edge off. Nothing wrong with that, but it's unusual for me.

For part of the first trimester, sex was far from my mind. Sort of hard to feel turned on when you're puking and frantically trying to avoid the smell of mushrooms in the grocery store. Also, it's hard to crave sex when you're overwhelmed by your cravings for cheesecake.

This does not mean I never thought about sex during the first trimester. I did, especially when Vince was around.

But now, it's a whole different story.

Sex. Sex. Sex.

I swear there's a neon sign in my brain, flashing that single word.

And now it's Friday, and I have another date with Vince.

I told myself I wouldn't sleep with him yet, and I managed to restrain myself last week, even though he was so sweet and incredibly good-looking.

This time, however, I'm not sure I'll manage it.

Just the thought that he'll be here any minute is sending me into overdrive. My skin is flushed. My nipples are unbearably sensitive. I want to strip off my clothes and greet him naked.

No! Don't do it!

I'm wearing a flowery summer dress, even though it's only April, but today is the warmest day so far this year, and my body's temperature regulation has gone haywire. The dress is low-cut, and I think it does a great job of showing off my boobs, which are bigger than usual thanks to the baby. Apparently he or she is now the size of an orange.

The phone rings, and I buzz Vince up.

By the time I open the door, I'm practically jumping out of my skin.

Vince, of course, looks ridiculously handsome. When does he not? He leans against the doorframe and smiles at me, hands in his pockets.

Something's a little off, though. There's a faint shadow under his eyes that isn't usually there.

But when I smile at him, he smiles back, nice and slow, and I get even more aroused. I have to stop myself from squeezing my thighs together.

Unfortunately, I don't stop myself from saying, "You look scrummy!"

"Uh," he says.

"Sorry, I've been watching too much of *The Great British Bake Off.*"

Yeah, I've been binge-watching it lately, although all the food makes me drool and I can barely stand the fact that I can't taste any of it.

"You do look really good," I say.

"Thanks."

"I should warn you that I'm very horny."

"Oh, you, too?" he murmurs.

Man, he's so suave and cool, and I'm anything but. I'm usually nowhere near this bad, but, you know…Vince Fong and pregnancy.

"I have a good excuse," I say, lifting my nose in the air.

"Me, too. I haven't had sex since January."

"Same here. That's only a few months. A few months is nothing."

His eyes widen. "It sure doesn't feel like nothing to me."

"My good excuse is pregnancy hormones, something you aren't experiencing."

"True, I'm not."

He's wearing a short-sleeve shirt today, so I have a good view of his forearms. Have I ever found forearms this sexy before?

"How are you so calm right now when I want to climb you like a tree?" I ask.

He smirks at me.

My God, he's infuriating.

He takes a step toward me and tips up my chin. His gaze isn't pointed at my face, however. No, he's making a show of staring down my dress, which I don't mind.

"Let's go out for dinner," I say.

"Are you sure? Seems like you're itching to get out of that dress."

He steps even closer, until we're toe-to-toe. He brushes his hand over my hip, and I gasp.

"You want to know what I do when I'm alone?" he asks.

I'm already developing a picture in my mind, without him saying anything.

"Sometimes when I'm in the shower," he says. "Sometimes when I'm in bed. I grasp my cock…you miss doing that, don't you?"

"Yes," I groan before I can help myself. We only had one weekend together in bed, but I miss doing that. So much.

The corner of his mouth quirks up. I want to wipe that stupid smile away by pushing him down between my legs and telling him to lick me, like he did at the party.

But I don't.

"And I think of you, Marissa," he says. "It's always *you*. Your wet heat surrounding me. Your fingernails scratching my back so hard they leave marks."

I cross my arms over my chest. "I did not do that."

I try to sound firm, but perhaps he's telling the truth. I can't be sure, not when my mind is turning to mush and that giant SEX! sign seems even bigger than before.

"And I jack myself off," he continues. "Way more than usual. Because I can't stop thinking of being with you again."

"How interesting," I murmur, managing to channel his calmness.

"Very interesting, I agree." He waits a beat. "Are you sure you'd like to head to dinner now?"

"Yes."

See? I have self-control.

"As you wish," he says, stepping out of my personal space.

"Where are we going? A sausage factory?"

He barks out a laugh.

This time, he doesn't take me out for drinks beforehand, and the Middle Eastern restaurant is only a short distance away. We order muhammara for our appetizer, and we both get lamb kebabs for our main. There are, indeed, sausages on the menu, but I refuse to make a comment about it.

When the muhammara arrives, I immediately break off a piece of pita and swipe it through the dip. Roasted red pepper, walnut, and pomegranate molasses. It's delicious and has the perfect hint of sweetness.

I eat half of the muhammara in a hurry, and then I watch

Vince. He's eating slowly, probably to torture me. He tears off some pita with his fingers…those fingers that could be inside my body. His lips, wrapping around the food…his mouth could be on my nipple, or my clit, or my earlobe. So many possibilities, and I want all of them.

"You okay, Marissa?" he asks, and I'm positive he can read my mind.

"Just peachy."

"Here, you can have the rest." He slides the dish over to me.

All I care about right now is food and sex. Honestly, nothing else in the world matters.

I eat the rest of the appetizer.

It's good, but not as good as sex.

Our main course is good, too, but I have the same problem. I dip a piece of lamb in the yogurt sauce, and yes, that's excellent.

But not as excellent as sex.

Vince places his hand on my knee and slips his fingers under the hem of my dress.

"You bastard," I mutter as I lean forward so I can also touch his knee.

It strikes me as slightly ridiculous. We're at a restaurant with delicious food on the table in front of us. We can't really *do* anything to each other here.

And yet.

I help myself to some rice. That's what's important right now. Food. Providing myself with nourishment for a wild evening of sex.

No! I'm not supposed to sleep with him.

Okay, it's time to be honest with myself. I'm going to sleep with him. I'm super horny and he's very willing and extremely hot.

I can handle this, though. I'm just craving him because I'm pregnant, right? We can sleep together—it's a sensible thing to do. I was scared that sex would change things and there would be no going back, and I'm still not sure what I want beyond tonight...but I was wrong to worry. It's only sex; we've done it before. It doesn't have to *mean* anything.

"What are you thinking about?" Vince asks.

I stab a piece of pepper. I don't want to give him the satisfaction of knowing I've decided to sleep with him.

He rubs circles over the inside of my knee with his thumb, and I clench my thighs.

"Oh, nothing," I say as I continue to eat. The food really is good, but not as perfect as it would feel to have Vince inside me...

I squirm in my seat and try to swallow my moan, but I don't quite manage, and Vince spears me with one of his sexy-as-all-get-out grins.

If I hadn't already decided to sleep with him, that would have done the trick.

"What did you have planned for after dinner?" I ask, trying to act all cool. "Another bar with good mocktails?"

"No," he says.

Oh, thank God! We can go back to my place and have sex!

"It's a nice night, isn't it?" he continues. "It's finally starting to feel like spring. There's a gelato place near St. Clair...why don't we mosey down there after dinner? We could also stop for some tea—"

"Vince." I grit my teeth.

"Why, whatever is the problem, Marissa?" He rubs his thumb a bit higher, and I practically beg him to drop to his knees and put his mouth on me.

However, we're in a restaurant. The tables on either side of us are occupied, and someone would almost certainly notice. Although maybe, if he's really stealthy...

No, someone would definitely notice, especially since I wouldn't be able to keep quiet.

"You bastard," I mutter again.

As payback, I pull down the neckline of my dress, just a little, and his eyes are, predictably, drawn to my cleavage.

Good. Two can play this game.

The waiter comes to clear our plates. "Would you like to see our dessert menu?"

"Sure, let's take a look," Vince says, annoyingly smooth. He touches my hand. "What do you think, honey?"

"I think we should get the bill," I say decisively, looking at the waiter. "Please."

He nods and brings it over two minutes later.

This time, I don't argue over who's going to pay the bill. That would be a waste of precious time. Instead, I let Vince use his credit card, and then I tug his hand and march out of the restaurant with him trailing behind me.

"Where are you going, Marissa?" he asks. "In a rush for something?"

"It's your fault."

"Mine?" He has the nerve to sound affronted.

"For looking so goddamn sexy! For knocking me up and making me feel so horny!"

"I do apologize."

I stop walking and turn to face him, hands on my hips. "How are you so composed right now? I thought you were horny, too."

"I am. It's taking every ounce of willpower in my body—and I'm not accustomed to using my willpower—to stop myself from pushing you up against that brick wall and having my way with you." He points to the side of a building. "Your tits look magnificent in that dress, as I'm sure you're aware. But I think it would be best to wait until we get back to your condo, and besides, it's fun to watch you squirm and get pissed at me."

"I hate you."

"No, you don't. Because when we get to your bedroom, I'm going to make you feel really, really good." He presses a kiss to the side of my neck. "I'm going to slide my fingers into your pussy…"

God, I can't stand this anymore. I drag him toward the car, and ten minutes later, we're pulling up to my building. After he helps me out, he pushes me against the car door and sticks his tongue down my throat. I moan.

"Shall we take this upstairs?" he asks.

"Yes," I say. "I want you."

And I think I can have you without it meaning anything.

As soon as we stumble, sober, into the entryway of my unit, we're on each other again. Mouths clashing, hands roaming. He hitches up the bottom of my dress and slides his hand beneath my underwear.

"I wore a dress today for easier access," I tell him.

"Excellent forethought."

"I'm annoyed you can still use words like 'forethought' right now."

"It's just the way I am, I have a superior intel—*ohhh.*"

I smile. Finally, I feel like I have the power. My hand is down his pants, wrapped around his cock. Although to be honest, it's kind of difficult to think when I'm touching him so intimately and anticipating how it'll feel to have that inside me.

His fingers are good, don't get me wrong. He slides one inside me, and I tip my head back. He takes advantage of that and presses kisses to the underside of my jaw.

In return, I begin stroking my hand up and down.

"Better than doing it yourself?" I ask.

"A zillion times better."

"Great use of scientific terms."

"Thank you. I do my best."

He pushes aside the short sleeves of my dress and shoves down my bra to reveal my breasts. They pebble in the cool air and in expectation of his touch.

He sets his mouth to one nipple as he pulls out a condom

from his pocket, and I almost weep in relief. It's a good thing he tears open the condom package—my hands are shaking so much, I'm not sure I'd be able to do it.

He lifts me up and brings me down, impaling me on his cock.

I groan.

He groans.

This is what we both wanted for so long. All through dinner… and for much longer than that. I *need* this, this sense of fullness that seems to complete me. I'm finally getting relief from something other than my toys.

I cling to him as he walks toward my bedroom, continuing to move me up and down on his cock. He sets me down on my bed, on my back, never breaking his pace. When he swipes a lock of sweaty hair back from my forehead and smiles at me, I feel like I'm about to shatter.

"Vince," I murmur, burrowing my head against his shoulder.

"I know," he says. "I know."

He slams into me again. He's so powerful. So perfect. I feel like I'm about to combust…and then he touches my clit, and I do. I sob and shake and cry out and hold onto him with everything I've got until he finds his own release.

He pulls out of me and disposes of the condom, and I almost sob again at the loss.

When he returns to the bedroom, I wrap my arms around him, not wanting him to go anywhere. "I hope that wasn't enough for you."

"Nowhere near enough," he assures me. "We're just getting started. Do you regret insisting we go out for dinner first?"

"A little, but it was probably for the best. I would have gotten hungry at some point."

"And sent me down to Cheese & Me for matcha double fromage cheesecake?"

"Fortunately, I have some in the freezer."

"Well, that's a relief. Didn't want to bribe any teenagers again."

"How horrible that must have been for you."

"You know," he says, "we do have a bit of a problem."

"And what would that be?"

"You're still wearing clothes."

"Oh. So I am."

They're not on properly anymore, but I am indeed wearing clothes. I let Vince pull my dress over my head, followed by my bra. Next, he takes off my panties. When he was inside me, he merely pushed them to the side.

I wore nice ones today. Even though I told myself I wouldn't have sex with him...well, I couldn't help thinking about it.

Once my clothes are off, I get to work on his. It's been a while since he's been gloriously naked in bed with me, and damn, it's nice.

But what if...

No. We're just having sex because we're both in desperate need of sex. Why should we deny ourselves? We're good in bed together and he treats me well.

He rests his hand on my stomach, and it feels possessive.

"What should we call the baby before they're born?" he asks. "Lime?"

"Lime? Why?"

"Because that's how big they were at the first ultrasound."

"Would we call them something different each week as they grow? Like, they're now about the size of an orange, so..."

He chuckles.

"I just call them Baby," I say. "Nice and simple."

"Okay, I can do that." Vince rests his cheek on my stomach. "Hi, Baby. I'm your father, and I'm so excited to meet you."

Oh, God. The stupid hormones are making me teary-eyed.

I can almost see us living together. The fact that he proposed to me...it doesn't seem quite as ridiculous now, and I believe that being an important part of the child's life isn't just a passing fancy for him.

I'd convinced myself that going to bed with him didn't have to involve feelings, didn't have to change anything. But it's so intimate, lying here next to him, talking about our baby.

Still, we've only been on two real dates, and I'm only just getting accustomed to the idea that being with him, really being with him, is a possibility.

"Don't worry," Vince continues, still speaking to my stomach, "We'll change your name once you're born. Baby is an odd name. Though there's a movie about a girl who goes by 'Baby.' It's called *Dirty Dancing*."

"Have you seen it?" I ask.

"Of course. My mom was a little in love with Patrick Swayze, and when my dad was annoying her, she'd threaten to leave him for Patrick. Did you hear that, Baby? Your grandma likes Patrick Swayze. Unfortunately, you won't get to meet him because he's dead, but maybe she'll make you watch his movies with her one day. I'll do better things with you, though. I'll give you a bloopisaurus, and you can name him whatever you want. Or if you prefer princesses and fairies, that's okay, too. I can make you a little princess tower for your room. Not that I know anything about construction, but your mom's an engineer. She's really smart, did you know that?"

I think Vince could talk to Baby forever, but he can do that later. I want him to pay attention to *me*.

I pull him up and wrap my arms around him. My skin against his.

When I kiss him, open-mouthed, he slides his hand between my legs again. Why does it feel so amazing when he touches me? Does every woman who sleeps with him feel like this?

I push those thoughts out of my head. *I'm* the one he's dating. *I'm* the one who's carrying his child.

He plays with me leisurely, his finger brushing my clit, parting my folds.

"I got tested after I found out I was pregnant," I say, "just to be sure. And you?"

"I can show you my test results from March. I promise I haven't been with anyone since then."

He starts to get up, but I lay a hand on his shoulder.

"I trust you," I say. "I trust that you had the tests and they came back clear, and I trust that you haven't had sex since January. Since I'm already pregnant…" I roll on top of him and rub myself against the underside of his cock.

"Fuck," he says.

"Don't swear around Baby," I say lightly. "So, do you want to do it without a condom? I want to feel you come inside me." God, I do. I can't help *wanting* when we're naked together like this.

I rub myself against him again.

"Yes," he rasps out. "Fuck, yes."

I don't admonish him for swearing this time. Instead, I grin.

He reaches between us and positions his cock at my entrance. I take him easily.

It's been a long time since I've ridden a man bare. I've certainly never done it with a man who wasn't my boyfriend, but this is Vince, and he's in a special category of his own.

We move in unison, our movements slow and deep. I feel almost painfully close to him.

I lean over and kiss his neck, then his mouth. He breaks the kiss so he can suckle on my nipples. He fills his hands with my ass and squeezes.

As good as this is, I know it won't be enough for tonight. I'll want him again and again, and he'll take me.

He picks up the pace, and I cry out just a moment before he does.

He stays inside me until he starts to go soft, and I love lying here under his weight.

"You were magnificent," I tell him.

"You were pretty good yourself."

"Just pretty good?"

"Don't want it to get to your head."

"I think you're the one with the big ego, not me."

"Me?" he says. "Never."

He pulls out of me slowly, and I slide my fingers inside.

"Can you grab that towel?" I ask, and Vince gets the towel on the rack beside the bed. I place it under me.

Eventually, we make it to the washroom to clean up, and he fucks me again while I'm sitting on the bathroom counter, something he admits he's fantasized about.

By midnight, we're back in bed together, cuddled up and sated...at least for a little while. He falls asleep first, and I lie quietly beside him, listening to his breathing, reveling in the soreness between my legs, wondering if having sex with Vince tonight was the best idea.

I couldn't help myself, though. I wanted him so badly.

But I'm not ready for everything he's prepared to give me. If I weren't pregnant, this would be so much simpler. I wouldn't feel like I had to figure out everything quickly.

Except this baby will be coming in less than six months. I like Vince, but there are already so many changes in my life. And while he's been sweet to me—when he's not trying to push my buttons—I'm still having a bit of trouble reconciling that version of Vince with the one the rest of the world knows. I trust him, I enjoy his chats with our baby, but I feel like I don't know him completely.

For now, though, sex has left me tired, and my mind is emptying of thought.

[20]

VINCE

"Maybe I should not say anything." Marissa's mother, Bev, helps herself to some noodles. "I usually wouldn't, but this time, I will say it anyway."

Marissa and I exchange an oh-shit look.

"See, that's what I'm talking about," Bev says. "You act like you are a couple, but you are not, right?"

We're at Marissa's mother's home for Sunday dinner. Up until an hour ago, the weekend had revolved around sex, and we didn't talk about this dinner with Bev and Larry. Or about where our "relationship"—can I call it that?—is headed.

I'm tempted to tell the truth. Not the truth about what we were doing all weekend, but something along the lines of, *I love your daughter, and we've started seeing each other.*

However, I don't know what Marissa told her mother in the past and what she wants to tell her mother now. I don't wish to go against what she wants.

Marissa remains quiet, though, so perhaps I ought to say something.

"You're not like my family," I tell Bev. "They love to interfere, and they will always speak, even if it would be better for them to keep their mouths shut."

Admittedly, I'm like that, too. Especially with Julian. But there are some things I don't talk about with my family.

Bev chuckles, then does something I was dreading.

She speaks to me in Cantonese and shoots me a smile afterward.

Even though I was prepared for this moment, I find myself unable to form words.

"He doesn't speak Cantonese," Marissa says.

I never told her that, but it's obvious I don't.

"Right, I remember now," Bev says. "Your family is Toisanese, yes?"

I nod. "But I don't speak it. My parents were born here, and they're most comfortable speaking English. They didn't make a point of speaking Toisanese at home, and there are no classes for that. They put us in heritage language classes for Cantonese instead, but…" I shrug. "All the other kids spoke it at home, and the class was mainly for learning to read and write. So I was lost the whole time. My older brother picked it up, but I'm terrible at languages."

"It is just surprising because your family is…" She gestures vaguely.

I know what she means. I come from a well-known family in the Chinese community, yet it's hard for me to really feel like part of the community when I speak none of the languages. I don't speak Mandarin, either.

I sort of wish I could speak *something*. But I'm third generation on my mom's side, fifth on my father's. I wasn't interested when I was younger, and I really am bad at languages. French was always my worst subject in school.

I'm not ashamed of my Chinese background, though, and it's not like I tried to reject everything Asian and hang out with only white people.

"Will you teach your baby Cantonese?" Bev asks Marissa.

"I haven't thought about it yet."

"I would like to speak to them in Cantonese. We will see each other lots and they will learn to at least understand it. But you tell me what you would like. You are the mother."

Yeah, her mom is definitely different from mine.

"Back to you two," Bev says. "Marissa said you proposed?"

Oh, she mentioned that to her mom?

"Yes," I say, "and that offer still stands."

Marissa glances at me but says nothing.

"So, Vince," Larry says, "I hear you ran a tech company. What do you do now?"

I reach for the scallops. "A little of this, a little of that."

As in, I plan dates for Marissa and see my family and listen to my friends' shock when I tell them I want to settle down.

I was feeling particularly useless this morning. While Marissa was sleeping, I went to GoFundMe and donated a bunch of money to families struggling with medical bills and rent money, thinking of what Marissa had told me about her life growing up. How much difference money I might call "pocket change" could make to someone.

"A man should have a purpose in life," Larry says.

"I agree."

I'm not sure whether Larry is the sort of old-fashioned guy who'd consider family a reasonable purpose in life for a woman, but not for a man.

"If you do not get married," Bev says, setting down her chopsticks, "please do not make problems for Marissa when it comes to child support. I don't know how it all works, but you and your family could tie stuff up in courts with your money and connections, and we are nobody."

"There will be no issues. You have my word."

We eat in silence for a minute, and I'm feeling out of my depth. Meeting the mother of the woman who's having my baby and has yet to accept my proposal is a situation I've never been in before. I'm usually good at keeping the conversation going, but I don't have practice at getting people to see I could be a loving and responsible family man.

I don't seem to have done too bad of a job, however, because after we have almond cookies for dessert, Bev says she has something to show me and gestures for me to follow her to the basement.

"These are baby toys," she says, pulling out a box from one of the shelves. "From when Marissa was little. I don't know if she will want to use them, but you can give this to her."

"Why don't you do it?" I ask.

"Ah, I want to encourage her to develop tender feelings for you."

Well, perhaps she likes to interfere as much as my mother after all.

"I see the way she is looking at you," Bev says. "She told me before that she does not love you, but maybe she is changing her mind."

I try not to grin at those words.

"And I don't know, but you seem okay."

"Thank you for the high praise."

She laughs. "I was a bit worried, I won't lie. Marissa has good taste in men, though. If she wants you to be in her life and the baby's life, I'm sure you deserve it. But I like the idea of you being married—better for everyone, I think." She takes a mobile out of the box. It appears to be Winnie-the-Pooh and his friends. "Her father made this for her. She told you about him?"

"She did."

Bev nods but doesn't say anything for a moment.

"You will have to pick up the box later," she says, "to keep it a secret from Marissa. Then you can give it to her when the time is right. Can you visit on Wednesday?"

~

That night, I stay at Marissa's again. I'll leave in the morning when she goes to work, but for now, we're here together for the third night in a row, and I can't help smiling.

We had sex when we got home from visiting her mother, and now we're lying in bed, our legs entwined.

"I still don't get why you proposed as soon as I told you about the baby," she says. "You barely knew me then. Why did you do it?"

"I wanted—still want—us all to be a family together." I lace my fingers through hers.

"I know. It just seems out of character for you. Less so now that I know you better, but you know what your reputation is, and to propose to me right away..."

"The truth," I tell her, "is that I've been pretty unfulfilled lately."

"The parties, the drinking, the women, the special gummies— that's not a fulfilling life?"

"After I burnt out and sold the company, that's all I wanted to do. But with every passing year, my life started to feel more and more pointless. In some ways, I became less of a mess, but I still wasn't doing anything of meaning. It felt like I had no value."

"Vince," she says, "your life has value."

She strokes my face. I want to look her in the eyes, but it's too much right now.

"And then you told me you were pregnant," I say, my voice a little hoarse, "and it was like everything just fell into my lap. I hadn't known exactly what I wanted before, but suddenly I knew, and I can be a little impulsive."

"I'm glad you want to be a big part of our child's life. I thought you'd be the fun dad who'd come around a few times a month, and I was okay with that, because it was more than I had. I would have loved to have that much. This is better, though. And you and me…"

My heart is thumping wildly. What she says next seems of vital importance.

"I'm glad we're seeing each other, and not just because my hormones are out of control and you're providing me with sex. Though you do a pretty bang-up job of that." She absently runs her hand over my chest. "I know I was doubtful at the beginning, but I believe in your commitment now. I trust you."

"Thank you," I whisper, my voice a bit rough.

Several months ago, I never would have imagined that a woman saying *I trust you* would mean so much to me, but it does.

"And I can see you devote yourself to one thing at a time. You did nothing but work for years, and then you did nothing but cultivate your playboy image. Now, I worry you're counting on me and the baby to be your whole life. Like we're supposed to save you and define who you are. Which is not what I worried about before, but I do now. Yes, I know this baby is going to consume my life for a while, but other things are important to me, too. Like my job. Like watching *The Great British Bake Off* while enjoying a glass of wine and a slice of cheesecake."

"And I will take Baby for a nice long walk so you can have your time alone. I know that's important."

"Yeah, and I believe you." She pauses. "I'm not going to tell you to do the kind of work you used to do, but I just feel like you need more."

"I'll still see my friends on occasion, and I have the rest of my family."

"But from what I know of you, you need something else. Are you involved in your father's Toronto Chinese Canadian Center?"

"I give some money, but that's all. It's important work, but it's not really my thing. As you might have been able to tell, I have a rather uncomfortable relationship with the Chinese community here. I feel a little removed from it."

"Does that bother you?"

"On occasion."

It's strange to have a serious talk about my life with someone. Most of the conversations I have are not at all serious. Kidding around. I can do that with Marissa, too, but I appreciate this.

"Maybe you could think about changing that," she says. "Though I understand how you're quite far from the immigrant experience, and that's a lot of the focus of your family's organization. If you hated being Asian, I'd say you need to work on changing your attitude, but that doesn't seem to be the case. I'm not sure what you should do, but you're clearly intelligent and I think you'll be happiest if you find another outlet. You're lucky. You don't need money, and you have the time and resources to do whatever you want."

But how am I supposed to know what else I want?

"You and Baby are the most important things to me." I take her hand.

"That's fine," she says. "It doesn't need to be anything *big*. Though I think it would be good if you could give back. Just the thought of me and the baby being your whole life, well, it's a lot of pressure, you know?"

I nod.

She gives me a smile and turns over so her back is against my chest. I wrap my arms around her and feel content yet a little on edge at the same time.

"You thought you'd come to love me," she says, and I think she purposely didn't want to see my face for this. "Have you?"

"Yes."

I hold her close and kiss her neck. I do love her, and I admire the way she's level-headed and balanced, things that no one ever says about *me*. She's got the "normal" life that I never really imagined having, but now, it has an appeal I didn't understand before.

I wait for her to say she loves me, too, but she doesn't.

She cares for me and trusts me and takes me seriously, though…and that's a lot more than before. She also enjoys having me in her bed again.

It bugs me that she can't say it back, but I have hope that will soon change.

[21]

MARISSA

The following Sunday, Vince picks me up at five to take me to his parents' for dinner.

I'm wearing a dress, which had not been my initial plan, but the pants I'd planned to wear aren't very comfortable now. So, dress it is.

His parents live near the Bridle Path. We pull up to a brick house that isn't as grand as the newer gray stone homes flanking it on either side, but it's still a million miles from the apartment in Scarborough where I spent my childhood.

"This is where you grew up?" I ask Vince as he pulls into the driveway.

"We moved here when I was two or three, yeah."

There are three garage doors—three!—landscaped gardens, and a large tree in the front yard. The branches are bare now, but soon, it'll be covered in green leaves.

"I'm nervous." I hadn't meant to tell him that, but there it is.

"Don't worry. They'll love you." Vince smiles at me. "You're very lovable."

"That's because you know what's under this dress."

"And I hope to enjoy it again tonight." He waggles his

eyebrows then leans across the console and puts his hand on my stomach. "Hi, Baby. It's time to visit your father's family! They're very excited to meet you."

Oh, man. This guy.

I always wanted the Fongs to be a part of my child's life, but I didn't think I'd see them often. But now, I'm starting to wonder if Vince will play another role in my life other than the father of my child, and that's partly why I'm nervous.

I've met a boyfriend's parents before, and I can handle that. This situation is a little different, though, because I'm pregnant and everyone knows it. Also, it must be more than a decade since he's brought a woman to meet his family.

Interesting that I've started thinking of Vince as my boyfriend.

"I should probably mention something." He runs his hand through his hair. "Shit, I should have mentioned it earlier."

I immediately stiffen. "What?"

"My father is suspicious of you."

"I thought you said everyone would love me."

"I mean, I think so, but he's the one I'm not sure about. He visited me a couple weeks ago and said he was worried you tampered with our birth control and were after my money or… something like that." Vince winces. "He also asked if we'd had a paternity test."

"If you want one," I say, gripping the strap of my purse, "I'm happy to do so, though I'm not sure when it can be done in vitro."

"No, you don't have to. I trust you. I know you never would have done that to me."

I understand how this must look to his father, but I can't help feeling annoyed.

"Why didn't you tell me earlier?" I wish I'd been prepared for this, though I appreciate Vince's faith in me.

"I was hoping Dad would change his mind, but he didn't, and

then I forgot until today. I now think he has to meet you before he'll change his mind."

When we get out of the car, Vince squeezes my hand, and we walk up the path to the double front doors. He steps inside without knocking.

"We're here!" he shouts as he takes off his shoes.

I don't see anyone, but from somewhere in the house, I hear, "No, Evie!" and laughter.

A minute later, a man walks into the front hall. It must be one of Vince's brothers, but they don't look much alike, and this man's default expression seems more serious than Vince's.

"You must be Marissa," he says. "I'm Julian. Nice to meet you."

We shake hands.

"We're all in the front room." He jerks his thumb to the right. "Evie just crawled for the first time, then tried to grab my beer."

"Oh, did she?" Vince laughs and turns to me. "Julian likes old man beer."

Julian merely gives him a look.

Vince leads me into a room where several people are seated on couches and on the floor. Everyone is staring at the baby.

"Come on, Evie," says a young woman. "Show Uncle Vince how you can crawl."

Evie looks unimpressed.

"I know what she needs," says a man—Vince's other brother, I assume. I think his name is Cedric. He places a bottle of Labatt 50 a few feet away from Evie.

Evie crawls toward it.

Everyone laughs.

An elderly woman gets up from an armchair and hobbles toward me. "I am Vince's po po." She places her hand on my stomach.

I'm sure this will happen more often as I get bigger, but the idea of people I hardly know touching my stomach is uncomfortable.

"Po Po!" Vince says. "Only I get to touch Marissa like that."

"Are you together now?" Po Po addresses this question to me.

"Yes," I say.

"Ah, you are going to get married! I knew it would be this way."

"We're not getting married yet," Vince says.

"But you are engaged?"

"No, we aren't engaged. Just dating."

"She's already pregnant, though." Po Po turns back to me. "You are giving me another great-grandchild and I am very happy about that. Hopefully this one will not have a taste for beer. Not that we are letting Evie drink it, but she is fascinated by the bottle."

I locate Vince's parents on the couch by the window. His dad seems to be watching me intently...or maybe that's my imagination. I head over to introduce myself, and they ask how I'm feeling.

I don't mention my constant urge to jump their son.

Vince leads me to a loveseat. He picks up Evie and sits next to me with her on his lap.

"This is Auntie Marissa," he says, and I smile at his use of "auntie." Evie's hand is curled into a little fist. "You want to give her a fist bump? Okay." He lifts her fist in my direction, and I bump it with my own. "Remember when I said you're getting a new cousin? Marissa is your new cousin's mother."

Evie smiles as though she understands everything. She has two teeth.

I have to admit, I'm moved by Vince's ease with the baby.

Julian brings over a plush Pusheen toy. "This is from Uncle Vince, right, Evie?"

Evie grabs it eagerly and babbles.

"That's right, you play with Pusheen, not my beer."

I feel like Julian is making a point of showing me that Vince cares for his niece, and I'm touched his family wants to make me think well of him.

Aside from his father, perhaps.

At the same time, as I look at Evie, I feel a little overwhelmed. Not that I haven't been around babies in the past few years—I have. My friends' children, for example. But this is the first time I've spent time with a baby since getting pregnant.

Soon, I'll have a baby of my own. I'll nurse her, change her diapers, comfort her when she cries, and give her baths… Or maybe it'll be a boy.

What on earth made me think I could do this?

But then Vince clasps my shoulder and gives me a smile. We're in this together. That makes me feel better.

And Evie giggles, and it's the sweetest sound.

"I'm Courtney, Vince's sister-in-law," says the woman sitting on the couch next to ours. She leans over, and we laugh when I'm just barely able to shake her hand without getting up from the loveseat. "Are you scared about being a mom for the first time?"

"A little," I admit.

"You can ask me questions anytime," she says, and I thank her.

"Where did you and Vince meet?" Julian asks.

"At a party." Or am I supposed to lie about that? I don't know.

"Of course you did. It's Vince, after all."

"Hey!" Vince says. "You met Courtney at a coffee shop—"

"Exactly. Not one of these wild parties you seem to fancy."

"—and offered her five thousand dollars to live at your place for two weeks and teach you how to have fun."

I bark out a laugh.

Then I realize nobody else is laughing and Vince is serious.

He turns to me. "She convinced him to do shocking things like read on the balcony in the middle of the day with a beer."

"You got that phallic cactus, too," Cedric says.

"I looked up what this 'phallic' word means." Po Po sniffs. "I do not approve."

"Don't worry," Vince says. "Joey is not very phallic anymore. His, uh, balls have gotten quite big and he's not as erect."

"Maybe we should talk about something else," Vince's mom says, "so Marissa doesn't think we're too weird."

Evie squawks loudly.

"Yes, you must be careful," Po Po says, "or Evie's first word will be 'phallic cactus.'"

"That's two words," Julian mutters.

"You know what I mean! It is bad language for a child, and they always copy the worst things they hear."

"Like how Vince's first two-word phrase was 'fucking asshole.'" His mom turns to her husband. "Thanks to your road rage."

"It set the tone for the rest of Vince's life," Cedric says, and Vince gets up to swat his brother. Cedric allows this, but then steals Pusheen.

Evie immediately starts wailing.

"Guess what I found in the basement the other day?" Vince's mom says. "General Bloopy." She holds up a rather sad-looking purple dinosaur.

"General Bloopy the Second," Vince says morosely. "I can't believe you lied."

"Not my fault you couldn't tell the difference." She holds the dinosaur toward the loveseat. Vince grabs it and hands it to Evie.

She isn't comforted.

"See?" Vince says. "She knows he's a fraud!"

"Come here, love." Courtney picks up her daughter and snuggles her. "It's okay. Mama will get your Pusheen back from Mean Uncle Cedric."

"I'm not mean!" Cedric protests, and Vince snorts.

My attention is ping-ponging between all the members of Vince's family, trying to follow the conversation, the affectionate teasing.

"Do you have much family here?" Vince's mom asks.

I shake my head. "Just my mother, plus her husband and his family."

"So you have a stepfather?" Po Po asks.

"I don't think of him as my stepfather. I didn't meet him until I was in my late twenties."

"What about your father?"

Vince gives his grandmother a look.

"He's dead."

Always a great conversation killer. Ever since I was little.

I glance at Vince's father. What would it be like to have Charles Fong as a dad?

This is the family I yearned for as a child. At Christmas, most of the other kids would have family to visit—grandparents, aunts and uncles, cousins—or siblings to play with.

But not me.

When I was four, I told my mom I wanted a sister for Christmas, and I still remember the uncomfortable silence, the way her lip trembled. I gave her a hug because clearly I had upset her—not that I understood why—and it seemed like the right thing to do.

Now I know that having a big family doesn't mean you'll have good relationships with them, doesn't mean they're people you can count on.

But I like Vince's family so far.

"You okay?" he whispers.

"Yeah, I'm good."

He's grabbing Pusheen back from Cedric when a middle-aged woman appears at the door to the room.

"Dinner is ready," she says.

Okay, this family is a little different from the one I imagined as a kid.

They have a chef.

[22]

MARISSA

AT DINNER, Julian and Charles ask about my job, and I'm pleased to talk about something other than my pregnancy. I don't say, *I'm not planning to live on Vince's money*, but I emphasize that I expect to return to work after a year.

I understand his father's protectiveness, I do. I can't help wishing I had a father to feel protective about me. From what I know about my father, he wouldn't have gone overboard, and that's good. He wouldn't have threatened a boy for daring to so much as look at me.

But I can't be sure.

How can I miss my dad when I don't remember him? When this is the life I've always known?

I didn't have a bad childhood. I had a great mom. She wasn't around as much as she wanted to be, but I always knew she loved me.

If Vince and I have a girl, what will he be like when she's a teenager? Will he freak out if a boy touches her shoulder? Would he worry about boys treating her the way he's treated girls?

But Vince was nice and respectful to me when I was a two-night stand.

God, I shouldn't be thinking about this now. I should be enjoying my food, which really is quite delicious. Especially these noodles. Mmm.

For dessert, there's a chestnut cake, which I haven't had in ages, but my mom used to get one each year for my birthday. I'd forgotten how much I like it. It's the kind of chestnut cake where the sweet, pureed chestnuts are in the shape of spaghetti. I think the correct term is Mont Blanc, but I always just called it "chestnut cake."

I compliment the cake, even though nobody in Vince's family made it, but I try not to gush. I don't want to seem uncool and awed by the simplest of things.

But I imagine that my child will enjoy chestnut cake—because my child will have excellent taste, of course—and celebrate birthdays with this family. Maybe I will be there, too?

The idea of me being with Vince long-term is still hard to envision.

After dinner, Courtney says, "Come with me."

I follow her, as does Vince.

"No, not you," she says to him. "Don't worry, we're just going to talk about you, the way you and me talk about Julian."

He laughs, but I can tell he's a little alarmed.

However, he lets me go with a look that says, *Come get me if you need anything.* We've been spending so much time together that we can communicate without words.

I look back at him for a moment, and when I turn to Courtney, she's chuckling.

She leads me to a room that's smaller than the one we were in before dinner. She sits on the couch and I take an armchair.

"How's the pregnancy going?" she asks.

"Not too bad. I'm just hungry all the time."

She nods sympathetically. "Has your morning sickness passed?"

"More or less, yeah."

She rests her elbow on the arm of the couch and puts her head in her hand. "What's Vince like in a relationship? I'm curious."

"Oh," I say. "He's nice."

"*Nice*. It's not the word people usually use to describe Vince, but I know what you mean. Kind of a bland description, though." She raises her eyebrows.

What does she want me to tell her?

"He took me out for mocktails, and he'd been to the place beforehand and tried half the menu so he could tell me what was good."

Courtney giggles. "Yeah?"

I start to relax. She doesn't want dirt on Vince, nor is she interrogating me to make sure I'm good enough for her husband's family. I feel younger than I am, like we're two girls giggling over boys.

"I always thought Vince just needed to meet the right woman," she says.

I hesitate. "I feel like I'm supposed to save him."

I'm glad I talked to Vince about it last weekend, but this is the first time I've voiced that fear to anyone else.

She tilts her head. "What do you mean?"

"Like, he wants me and the baby to be his whole purpose in life, and I'm afraid I'll disappoint him. I think he needs something in addition to taking care of us."

Courtney opens her mouth, but then Julian walks into the room, carrying Evie in a detachable car seat.

"Why, hello!" Courtney coos. "Is it bedtime?"

Evie makes a bunch of loud noises.

"That's okay," Courtney says. "Daddy will sing you a song, and you'll go right to sleep. You always say you won't, but you do. Usually, anyway."

Julian sits down in an armchair, Evie on the floor in front of him, and he leans over and starts singing to her in Cantonese.

Courtney watches them with a fond smile. Julian really is sweet with his daughter, and I'm sure she has him wrapped around her little finger.

He's singing something about a mosquito, then a cat.

And the weird thing is…I *know* this song.

I shut my eyes and try to remember. Someone sang this to me. I think it was a man's voice, though not as low as Julian's.

But there weren't any men who looked after me. There was just my mother, and two other women in the building who'd take care of me while she worked. The only man…

Oh my God.

I *remember* him.

I thought I only remembered his funeral, and everything else I'd reconstructed from what my mother told me over the years.

But I do remember my father.

I can hear his voice in my head. He sounds like he's singing with a smile on his face. It's not, objectively, as nice of a singing voice as Julian's, but it's my dad's, and it's such a precious thing.

Someone touches my leg. "Marissa, are you okay?"

I can't manage to respond to Courtney. I think I hear her get up, but I need to keep my eyes closed to hold onto this.

My mother never sang this song, I'm sure of it, and she never told me that he sang it. No, I remember this on my own.

The song ends.

"Sing it again," I say frantically.

Julian does as I request without asking why. I open my eyes just long enough to see that Evie is asleep, so this song is only for me.

Distantly, I'm aware that I just met my boyfriend's family for the first time, and here I am, tears streaming down my face. This isn't how meet-the-parents dinners are supposed to go.

But…

Baba.

I smile through my tears. I don't remember him looking at me over my crib; I can only hear his voice. Just this one song.

It means the world.

The memory is taking on some clarity. At first I was terrified I would forget it if Julian stopped singing, but now I know I won't. It will stay with me, and I will cherish it.

I'd just turned three when I lost my father. It wouldn't make sense for me to have memories from when I was Evie's age, but maybe he sang it to me up until the day he died.

Someone squeezes in beside me on the armchair.

"You okay?" Vince asks.

"He sang this to me," I say. "I remember now."

When Julian finishes the song, I still can't open my eyes, afraid of what I'll see. People watching me, wondering what on earth is going on. But Vince is here, and he knows who I'm talking about. We haven't spoken about it much, but he knows, I'm sure of it.

"I can't understand the words," Vince says softly, and I hear the smile in his voice, just like I could hear it in my father's voice. "I wish I did, but I don't."

"Did anyone sing it to you when you were little?"

"Not that I recall. I don't know where Julian learned it. But I'll sing it to Baby, okay?" He places his hand on my stomach.

"Okay," I say between sobs. "That would be nice."

We sit there for a few minutes, and he doesn't tell me to stop sobbing, just lets me cry against his shirt.

Eventually, he says, "You want to head out?"

I finally open my eyes. There's nobody else in the room, just me and Vince, and he's smiling at me uncertainly. I throw my arms around him.

Everyone appears by the door when we put on our shoes. They say it was nice to meet me, but I'm only dimly aware of my surroundings. My mind is focused on my father's singing voice and Vince standing next to me.

We walk down the driveway and climb into the car.

"I'm so glad I remember him," I say, even though I know I don't look glad about anything. I keep thinking of all that I missed, and it feels different than it did before.

When Vince starts driving toward my condo, I call my mother.

I know I'm right about this memory. Still, I want someone to confirm it for me, and there's only one person who can do that.

When she answers, I immediately say, "Did Dad sing this song to me when I was little?" Then I sing a couple lines and wait.

"Yes," she says. "You remember?"

"I remember."

"You loved it. I tried to sing it to you after he died, but you screamed every time. You knew it was the wrong person singing to you."

I think she's crying, but if I ask, she'll deny it.

"You met Vince's family tonight, didn't you?" she says.

"Yeah. When his brother sang that song to his daughter, I remembered and burst into tears."

My mother says soothing words to me. *I'm sure they understand. They must love you, how could they not?*

I end the call as we're pulling into the visitors' parking at my building. When we get out of the car, Vince opens the trunk and pulls out a box.

"What's that?" I ask.

"Some stuff your mother wanted me to give you." He pauses. "We can do it tonight. Or later, if you prefer."

"Tonight."

Upstairs, I open the box, and there's a small collection of toys I vaguely remember from my childhood, plus a mobile I don't remember at all.

"Your mom said your father made it," Vince says.

I smile at the slightly lopsided Winnie-the-Pooh characters. Then I close my eyes and conjure up my father's voice, trying to remember this mobile above my crib.

But I can't.

"You want to get ready for bed?" Vince asks, though it's only nine thirty and I never go to bed this early.

"Yeah."

He takes out a pair of pajama pants as well as a T-shirt. When I wear clothes to bed—which I don't always do when he stays the night—I alternate between my "pregnant and hungry" and "pregnant and cute" T-shirts. Vince picks the latter for me tonight.

"I should get a 'pregnant and hormonal' shirt," I mutter.

"Nah, this one is more appropriate."

I roll my eyes, and he chuckles.

He strips down to his T-shirt and boxers, and we climb into bed together. I snuggle up against him.

"Why did my mom give you that box rather than giving it directly to me?" I ask.

"To encourage you to develop tender feelings for me. Her words, not mine."

I snort, then grab a tissue. God, my nose is a mess.

But Vince is still here, and he holds me in his arms.

I'm no longer surprised when he's good to me. Deep down, he's kind and thoughtful. I'm not sure how he feels about people outside of his family knowing that, though he's certainly not hiding it around me.

"How was meeting my family?" he asks. "Before…you know."

"It was good. The family I never had."

"You can have them, too."

I swallow and burrow my face against his chest.

"They like you," he says.

"They'd like anyone you brought home because it hadn't happened in so long."

"You have a point, but…" He strokes my hair. "I love you, Marissa."

My heart fills with emotion, then empties.

I can't say it back.

I do like him very much, and I've said "I love you" to many men over the years, but I feel like if I say "I love you" to Vince, it has to mean forever.

I don't know why I feel that way, but I do.

And though we're having a baby together, it hasn't really been that long—I tell myself that's the problem. It hasn't been very long, and I don't truly know yet. I need more time.

But I'm starting to worry. I'm thirty-six, and I've had many decent relationships. I'm good at finding kind men and dating them...and then breaking up with them because my feelings aren't strong enough. I want a happy relationship that lasts years and years, but what if I just can't have that?

What if I'm incapable of it?

I can't return Vince's words, but I press myself against him and enjoy his comfort.

"I've never felt this way before," I say. "Nothing even close. Did you know that?"

Evie regards me seriously with her dark eyes and neither nods nor shakes her head.

"You don't believe me, Evie? I swear, it's true. I want to hold her for always and never let her go. And dammit, I really want to see my ring on her finger."

Marissa clearly likes me, but she won't tell me she loves me, and I'm practically frantic to hear her say it. I haven't pushed it; I shouldn't. But she means everything to me, and I can't stand the thought of never hearing those words from her lips.

And every bit of vulnerability she shows me…it intensifies my feelings.

When I held her last Sunday night, after meeting my family, after she heard Julian sing that song, I became even more desperate. I need her. I don't know how I'll manage otherwise. I need to sing our baby to sleep, then crawl into bed with Marissa.

I cannot bear the thought of any other future, and I no longer worry that my feelings won't last.

Yet sometimes, I still struggle to believe she can love me back.

What if there's something wrong with me that prevents it? I have little experience with this stuff, as everyone knows.

"Did you like Marissa?" I ask Evie.

She makes some incoherent noises.

"I'll have to stop telling you my secrets. You might repeat them to Mommy and Daddy."

"What might she repeat to Mommy and Daddy?" Courtney is standing at the door to the playroom, her hair wet and a towel draped over her shoulders.

"Phallic cactus," I say without missing a beat.

"Thanks, Vince."

Evie isn't paying attention to us. She's crawling toward Pusheen at the other end of the room. Pusheen is better than Labatt 50, of that I'm certain.

"Good job, Evie," I say.

Courtney sits on the floor beside me. "How's Marissa doing? After last Sunday?"

"She's fine. She feels badly that—"

"Oh, she shouldn't. We understand."

I texted Julian the next day to explain and to thank him, as Marissa asked me to do.

"I like her," Courtney says. "I like her for you. She seems very down-to-earth."

"Yeah."

"By the way, Naomi's husband got a couple books for Evie that I thought you'd like." She grabs them off the bookshelf.

Quantum Mechanics for Babies.

Baby Loves Coding!

I laugh. "These are awesome."

I had no idea such books existed. I add them to my mental list of things to get for Baby, and as luck would have it, I'll be walking by Indigo on my way home. I usually drive to Courtney and Julian's, but I have something to pick up in Yorkville today, which is in between my place and theirs.

Plus, it's a beautiful day out. It's spring, and any day now, it'll be cherry blossom season. Normally, I wouldn't care, but I've been checking the High Park Cherry Blossom Watch.

I might not be an expert on romance, but cherry blossoms are romantic, right?

My plan is coming together.

I sure hope it works.

When I walk into the lobby of my building, Brian is there.

"Hey, Vince," he says. "Thought if I came to pick you up, you might actually go out tonight. There's a party."

"Of course there is," I mutter.

But the truth is, I kind of want to go. I have no plans tonight. Marissa is hanging out with her friends, and we'll see each other tomorrow instead. We've been spending most of our time at her place lately, but tomorrow, I'll have her over for the first time since that fateful weekend.

"Sure," I say. "I'll go."

"Yeah?" He follows me to the elevator.

"Why not?"

"So this whole commitment to the woman who's having your baby—that's over now? I told you—"

"Brian," I snap as the elevator doors close behind us.

He startles. He's not used to me talking like that.

"I love Marissa and I know what I want," I say. "I'm not going to change my mind, okay? You got me to doubt myself last time, but you won't succeed this time."

"But you want to go out tonight."

"Being in a committed relationship doesn't mean I can't go to a party. I won't pick up a woman, but I can still enjoy myself. Have a few drinks. Shoot the shit. Be in bed by two."

"By two? Are you serious?" he says, pretending to be outraged.

I relax. This is more like it.

"I know, I know. So, what do you say we have a drink, then head out?"

When we get to my suite, I pour us each a bourbon.

Brian downs his in one gulp and pours himself another.

I start to feel a little on edge again. Sure, things are changing, but why can't we enjoy a drink together?

"What's up?" I ask.

He's wearing a pinstripe suit and his hair is styled the way it normally is, but Brian's actions usually have a grace or polish about them, and today, he looks a little vacant. Rough.

Our friendship might be based on superficial shit, and I haven't known him for years and years, but I can tell something is wrong and I do care.

"So you really love her," he says, shaking his head.

"I do."

He tosses back another drink.

"What the fuck, Brian? Why can't you be happy for me? We'll still be friends. Besides, you make friends easily. Or do you still not believe I love her? Here, I'll show you." I pull out the small box I just purchased and open it up.

"You asking me to marry you? Gee, thanks, Vince, I'm flattered."

"Come on, be serious."

"Well, if you truly meant it, I'd be flattered."

"As you should be. I'm awesome."

"You are," he says quietly, and a horrible suspicion grips me.

Oh, fuck.

"But you love her," he continues bitterly. "Not me. You're having a baby with her. Not me. I don't even want a baby."

"Nothing wrong with that."

"I know."

But we're dancing around the truth.

Brian picks up the ring and slides it onto his pinky. "You didn't get her a big one."

"She wouldn't want that. I know her."

He puts the ring back in the box. "I'm the idiot. The idiot in love with his straight friend. I didn't think you'd ever fall in love, and we'd continue to hang out together all the time. It wasn't what I wanted, but it was something."

I press my hands to my face. I never considered Brian falling in love with anyone—least of all me—just like he, and so many other people, never thought I'd fall in love. And yet…

"You deserve someone who returns your feelings," I say.

He snorts.

"What? Why wouldn't you deserve that?"

"My life feels pointless," he says.

"So did mine. Until I met Marissa."

God. I pinch the bridge of my nose. Maybe Brian and I could have had real, meaningful conversations about shit like this.

But now, he's told me he's in love with me, and I've told him I intend to marry someone else. I'd like to remain friends, but if that's too hard for him, I understand.

"You'll find someone," I say.

"Thanks, Pollyanna."

"At least you have good taste." Seems like an appropriate Vince Fong thing to say.

"I'd kiss another guy and wish you'd get jealous and push him out of the way."

"All those people you kissed and fucked. You were just hoping to make me jealous?"

"Oh, please. Don't get me wrong, I was enjoying myself. But at the back of my head, I did hope. Are you totally weirded out now?"

"No, just surprised."

Brian tosses back his bourbon and pours himself some more. "I threw so many parties because that's what you liked."

"I'm sorry."

He waves this away. "I should leave."

"You, uh, still want me to go to that party with you?"

"I think I'll head home instead."

Just then, I get a text from Cedric, who says he's stopping by since he's in the area. A minute later, there's a knock on the door.

Good timing, I guess?

Brian follows me to the door and puts on his shoes. The instant I open the door, I remember the last time I saw Brian, when he said he'd seen my brother at a café. *He's cute.* Knowing what I do now, I'm not sure what to think.

Brian mumbles a greeting to Cedric with none of his usual pizzazz and heads to the elevator.

Cedric stares after Brian.

"Who's that?" he asks once my friend has gotten in the elevator.

"That's Brian Poon," I say.

"You talk about him all the time, but I've never met him before."

Cedric is still looking toward the elevator.

I have pretty strong suspicions now, but I don't comment on them.

"Come inside," I say instead.

"How are you feeling today?" Vince asks me.

We're sitting at the counter in a hand-pulled noodle restaurant, watching the noodle maker slap the dough on his work surface.

"Good. Less overwhelmingly horny." I smile.

"Sounds horrible."

"No, it's a good thing. I can focus properly at work and don't think about sex whenever I see a banana…or let's face it, all the time." I sip my tea. "In fact, I'm not horny right now. Nope, not at all."

"You're full of shit," he murmurs. "We're sitting right next to each other, and your leg is pressed against mine."

The truth is that my hormones have felt more under control lately…when I'm not thinking about Vince. But I think about Vince a lot.

And he's right. Sitting next to each other like this, well, it does things to me.

I wish I could get to know him without obsessing about where this is going, but I'm seventeen weeks pregnant, and it feels like there's a countdown. By the time the baby comes, there needs to some level of commitment…or not.

I've still got a few months, but I need more time. Though I want this baby, the pregnancy also makes things complicated.

But I never would have given Vince Fong more than a couple nights if I didn't get pregnant, because he doesn't seem, outwardly, like my type.

I thought life was supposed to get more straightforward as you got older. Instead, I feel more confused.

The one thing that's straightforward, however, is that my body always responds to his.

He places his hand on my knee and slides the hem of my dress up the tiniest bit. I'm tempted to grab his hand and run out of here and head back to his place, but…noodles.

Vince rests his hand on my stomach. "How's Baby?"

"Baby is fine. About the size of a turnip."

He moves his hand back to my knee and leans in closer to whisper, "Turnip. Turnip."

"What are you doing?"

"Trying to see if I can turn you on just from saying 'turnip.'"

I stop myself from squirming.

"You claimed you weren't turned on from sitting next to me with your leg pressed against mine, but maybe this will work." He pauses for dramatic effect. "Turnip."

"It's not the word. It's the fact that your lips are against my ear and I can feel your breath."

"You're still getting turned on by me saying 'turnip.' And turnips aren't even phallic."

I snort with laughter as I squirm in my seat. I can't help myself. This whole conversation is silly, but he's so good at getting me turned on and making me laugh at the same time.

I'm about to whisper something equally dirty when the server places bowls of soup with beef and noodles in front of us. I sigh in bliss as the steam from the broth wafts toward my nose.

"You mentioned you've been here before?" I turn to Vince. "The sign out front says 'grand opening.'"

"I have, and it's good. That sign has been up for two years."

The noodles are, indeed, delicious.

Afterward, Vince sexily whispers "matcha double fromage cheesecake" in my ear, and I'm not sure whether he wants to go to Cheese & Me or to bed.

"I have another idea," I say. "There's a Japanese dessert place on Baldwin Street that I've been meaning to try. You want to go?"

"Sure," he says.

Carrie posted a bunch of pictures on Instagram, and OMG, they made me salivate.

I'm also very aware that soon there will be a baby, and going downtown to a dessert shop will be An Operation. In fact, as we approach the shop, I notice there's a set of stairs up to the front door, and it would be a pain to go here with a stroller. And maybe Baby would start screeching and I'd have to take my food to go.

But for now, it's just me and Vince and rows of delectable, cute desserts in a myriad of colors. I get a black sesame latte, and we order a slice of matcha yuzu cake to share.

It's just as tasty as it looks.

"Matcha yuzu cake," he whispers in my ear as we head outside.

"I've already had that," I say. "I'm not hungry for it."

Which is a lie. I'd eat it again in a heartbeat.

"Turnip," he whispers.

My God, why do the stupidest things make me giggle?

"Banana," he says. "One very large banana."

"Yellow with spots? Or green and firm?"

"Marissa, I want you."

"Can't imagine why, after what I just said."

"I know, it's a mystery to me, too." A smile plays on his lips, but his eyes are dark, and when he stops to cup my jaw and plant a kiss on my cheek, I feel like melting into the ground.

We go back to his penthouse, and just like the first time I was here, he immediately pushes me against the door—gently, though—and kisses me. He sticks his hand up my skirt and groans when he feels how wet I am from our inane whispering.

"Vince," I say, stepping back. "I have a question."

"Go ahead." He shoves his hands in his pockets, presumably to stop himself from touching me.

"It's something that's been bothering me for a while." Maybe I should have said this earlier, before he got me all hot and bothered.

"Okay."

"You've had a lot of sex partners. That number doesn't bother me, but I can't help worrying whether you'll be happy with just me long-term."

"You know I'll be faithful to you."

"I trust you, but will you be happy? Or will you miss, you know, other things? Orgies?" Never thought I'd be having this conversation with a guy, yet here we are.

"Being with you will make me happier than anything."

And there I go, feeling guilty again that I don't love him back.

"The only thing I could imagine," he says, "is doing those things with you, if you were into that."

"What do you mean?"

"When we met, I went down on you in a room full of people."

"They weren't watching."

"Some of them were. Regardless, we weren't alone. And if you want to do that again, well, I'd do it in a heartbeat. And if you want to fuck another man while giving me a blowjob, I could be into that, too. Or swapping, but only if we were in the same room."

I asked about what he wanted, but he's turned this into what *I* want.

To be honest, I tried not to think about the fact that I let him lick me in public, that I orgasmed in public. I wanted him so badly that I couldn't think about anything else. I wasn't ashamed I went home with a guy I hardly knew and spent the weekend with him, but I was a little ashamed of that part.

But maybe I'd like to do it again. Maybe I'd enjoy watching him with another woman, then taking his cock inside me after she comes. Maybe I'd enjoy two men touching me at the same time.

I've never done anything remotely like that.

My skin is burning up.

Vince grins at me, and I hate the space between us. I go to him, and a moment later, he's tossed my dress, bra, and panties on the floor.

"You like the thought, don't you?" he says. "I figured you might."

"Have you had threesomes?" I ask.

"Sure."

"Have you fucked two women, one after the other?"

"Yeah."

"Have you and another man taken turns with a woman?"

"More than two of us, sometimes."

I shut my eyes and imagine Vince and another man, taking turns with me.

Not long ago, we were talking about turnips, and now *this*.

The day we met, I wanted him to myself. But I do have fantasies. I always just considered them fantasies, to keep locked away and brought out with my vibrator. Perhaps they'll stay that way—or perhaps they'd be fun to explore within a relationship—but at least I can talk about them with him.

He kneels on the floor in front of me, still in his jeans and polo shirt, even though I'm nude. He pushes his finger inside and wipes my moisture on my leg afterward, showing me how wet I am.

"You have such a pretty pussy. Everyone would love to see it again." He sets his mouth on me, tracing my entrance, lapping up my moisture. Spreading my folds with his fingers. "They would know I was the luckiest guy in the room. And maybe, if he asked really nicely, you'd allow another guy to touch you, too."

With that, Vince stops talking and starts licking me with abandon. I press his head against me. I can't let him go. I need to come like this, and it won't take long. He works two fingers inside me, and I shudder.

When he licks my clit, my legs start to wobble. He eases me down until I'm lying on the floor, and then he's licking me again, his hands on my upper thighs, holding me open. God, I love seeing his head between my legs, and if there were other people in the room to watch…

I clench around him and cry out.

"Can you take my cock now?" he asks.

I nod. I'm unable to speak, overcome by that orgasm.

He carries me into the living room and spreads me out on the sofa with one leg hooked over the back. He doesn't undress, just opens his pants and slides into me.

Oh my.

His chest slaps against mine, over and over. Soon it'll be hard to have sex like this, I'll get too big, but for now…

Again and again, he pounds into me, taking me like he did that first night…and yet it's different now. We're not simply strangers who find each other attractive. So much has happened since then.

An ultrasound. Matcha double fromage cheesecake. Mocktails. Raspberry-balsamic sorbet. Crying to a lullaby. Turnips and conversations about threesomes.

God, our relationship is weird and wonderful.

"Marissa…I can't…" He quickens his pace, and a few strokes later, he comes inside me.

He doesn't pull out right away but takes my mouth in his and circles my clit with his thumb until I cry out.

"I love you," he says.

And that nearly ruins the moment because I still can't say it back.

But we're here. Together. Like that very first weekend.

We shower, and when I'm dressed in a robe that goes down to my ankles, he opens the door to a room I've never been in before.

There's a bassinet, a crib, a bouncer, a change table, a stroller, and a little dresser.

"Every item has been carefully researched and is extremely safe, don't worry," he says.

But I'm not worried, because of course Vince would do his research.

He took me to a great hand-pulled noodle restaurant, offered to fulfill my sexual fantasies, put together a crib…

And bought books called *Baby Loves Structural Engineering!* and *Baby Loves Coding!* He hands them to me now, followed by a book called *Rocket Science for Babies*.

I laugh. "Our child doesn't need to be a rocket scientist."

"Of course not. We'll love them no matter what. But these are cute, aren't they?"

How do I not love him? How can I not say it?

He's fallen for me quickly, even though he's inexperienced in the realm of love, and today, he's been perfect in so many ways, yet I can't do it.

Although he's not pushing me, I still feel the pressure.

He's said it multiple times, and the baby is coming. The timing of that can't be changed.

When I wake up at three in the morning, I can tell Vince isn't asleep, either. He's lying on his back—he usually sleeps on his side—with his hands behind his head.

"What are you thinking about?" I ask.

"Oh." He sounds surprised that I'm awake. "You can't tell Carrie."

"Okay."

"Brian is in love with me, and he hasn't taken it well that you and I are...you know."

"Brian is in love with you," I repeat. "How long have you known?"

"Thirty-four hours?"

"Does it bother you?"

"Of course. I hate that my closest friend is in love with someone who can't love him back. And I'm not sure if he wants to stay friends. Anyway..." Vince sighs. "Obviously this is harder for him than it is for me."

He holds me close, and we're quiet for a while. I have no sense of time. It could be five minutes, it could be an hour.

Soon, I'll have a baby to feed in the night. When I return to bed, will it be with Vince?

"What are you thinking about?" he murmurs.

"My dad," I answer automatically, even though it's not true.

But I have thought about my dad a lot recently.

I used to talk to him in my mind when I was falling asleep, tell him everything that was happening in my life. Imagine what he'd say in response.

And I've been talking to him as I fall asleep lately, though I hadn't done so in years.

But no, that's not what's keeping me awake.

"If I sing the song," Vince says, "will it help, or will it make you cry?"

"The latter."

He falls asleep a few minutes later, but I stay awake for a long time.

[25]

VINCE

IT'S A WARM DAY, and I don't need anything more than a T-shirt and jeans. When we exit the subway station, I put on my sunglasses and strike a pose.

"Don't I look cool, Evie?"

Julian is carrying Evie strapped to his chest, facing outward. I asked my brother about the carrier so I can order one for my collection of baby stuff.

Evie giggles. She seems in good spirits.

Courtney smiles, though she looks a little tired. Apparently, Evie is teething and keeps her parents up at night more than she has for months.

"A few years ago, you never would have taken a Friday afternoon off," I say to Julian. "You wouldn't have even left the office before seven."

"This is true."

"And now, here you are." I spread out my arms as we follow the crowds into High Park. "A romantic walk to see the cherry blossoms with your wife and baby."

Julian squeezes Courtney's hand then turns to me. "And my little brother."

"Yep," I say cheerfully. "Gotta make sure you stay out of trouble."

"Very funny. Usually you're the one trying to get me into trouble."

I shrug. "What can I say?"

That's me, the troublemaking younger brother.

And soon-to-be fiancé and father and family man.

The change in Julian is perhaps not as surprising as the change in me. Even six months ago, I never could have imagined this.

Though unlike him, I'm the sort of person who swings wildly from one thing to another.

"It's so pretty," Courtney sighs as we pass the first cherry tree with pale pink blossoms.

"It's not quite at peak bloom," I say.

"Pretty close."

Evie makes a squawk. Of agreement, I presume.

They have a point. It's close to perfect…just not quite perfect, and I want the best for Marissa.

"A few more might open by tomorrow morning," Julian points out.

We stop by a cherry tree. I hold up my phone and point it at Julian and Evie.

"Say 'phallic cactus!'" I snap a picture. When I put my phone down, I ruffle my niece's hair. "That would have been a great time for your first word, Evie."

The park is packed with people who have come to enjoy the Sakura trees for their brief bloom. As a group of Asian people taking pictures, we fit right in.

After a few more photos, we continue south.

"I'm glad you're not such a workaholic stick-in-the-mud now," I say to Julian. "It's nice to take an afternoon off, isn't it?"

He grunts. "Yes."

I stop walking. I feel a strange urge to tell him something I've never told him before. "I was the one who put the idea in Mom's head that you might burn out."

"Really."

"Yeah, and it was my idea for us to storm into your office—"

"Thank you for that."

"—and demand you take a two-week break. Underneath my fun, charming exterior, I really was worried. Because of my own experience, although you're more capable in many ways than I am."

He puts a hand on my shoulder. "You never let on that you worked so hard."

"I was trying to measure up to you. Not because I wanted to be more successful and beat you at life. Just because, well..." *You're my big brother, and I look up to you.*

"So you started a company and sold it for two hundred million dollars."

I shrug. "It seemed sensible. I would have held out for more money, but you know. I burnt out. Couldn't do it anymore."

He sighs heavily, as though he doesn't know what the hell to do with me, and pinches the bridge of his nose.

I smile.

"You made more money than I ever did," he says. "Then you ran in the other direction and started hanging out with Brian Poon."

I experience a slight twinge, but I try not to show it. "Yeah."

"Vince, when did you lose the ability to walk and talk at the same time? We're impeding the flow of pedestrian traffic."

Courtney laughs.

"Hear that, Evie?" I lean toward my niece. "Try saying 'pedestrian traffic.'"

"Ba," she says.

"Close enough." I pat her head. "Anyway, Julian, you should thank me for my interference, because now you have a wife and daughter. If we hadn't forced you to take time off—and if I hadn't tried to make you attend an orgy—you never would have met Courtney. See, I'm a genius."

"We're still not walking," Julian mutters, but he gives me a smile.

"And now I'm copying you again. Except, rather than being a successful businessman, I'm going to have a kid and wife. But don't worry, I very much want those things. I'm not doing it just to be like you."

"That's good," he says. "I'm glad you seem happier these days and less, uh, inclined to party until eight in the morning and throw up in my living room."

"I only did that once."

"Actually, you did it twice." He begins walking again, and I hurry to catch up. When I reach him, he touches my shoulder again and says, "Thanks." Then, "You'll do great."

"I know," I say, all cocky, but I really do appreciate his words.

We continue through the park, passing more trees, more people. Courtney takes lots of pictures and tips her face toward the sun. I keep my eyes peeled for the perfect location.

"What about here?" I say.

Courtney gestures to a row of portable toilets nearby. "You can do better."

"Right. Good point."

We walk down the hill to Grenadier Pond and spend a few minutes looking at a swan. Evie cries when Mean Daddy Julian tells her that she cannot ride it. She is comforted when Awesome Uncle Vince flips his sunglasses up and down to make her laugh.

We arrive at a smaller collection of cherry trees to the east, and I decide it's the right spot to bring Marissa tomorrow morning. We'll have to wake up early. We should probably be here by seven thirty or eight so it won't be too busy.

I don't need to propose in front of a giant crowd.

Courtney spreads out a picnic blanket and takes some pictures of Evie. After we eat gingersnaps and fruit, Julian and Courtney lie back on the blanket and look at each other like lovesick fools—not that I'm in a position to judge—while I play with Evie. I sit her down beside me, and she immediately crawls away at breathtaking speed and attempts to stuff a stick in her mouth. I pull her back and hold onto her.

There's a gust of wind, and petals fall from the trees like snow. Evie tries to slap them.

Next year, I'll be able to do this with Marissa and our own child. We don't know if it's a girl or boy yet, but we'll find out at the ultrasound next week, and I'll be happy either way.

I glance over at Julian and wonder if we'll have a second child. I like having siblings, but if Marissa doesn't want to do this again, that's okay.

Evie continues to play with petals and sticks, and Julian falls asleep, which he never would have done before. A nap! In the middle of the afternoon! My older brother supposedly stopped napping when he was six months old.

Courtney sits up. "This is a lovely spot, but are you sure it's the right time to propose?"

"Yes," I say sharply.

I understand why Marissa kicked me in the shin the first time I proposed to her, but now she's much more than a two-night stand. Now, we truly know each other, and I love her.

I think she loves me, too, even if she hasn't said so, and perhaps it's foolish, but Brian's feelings for me are reassuring. I don't want him to hurt—I hate that part—but now I know that my deep, dark fear of being unlovable is unfounded. Even when I was a bit of a mess, somebody did love me, somebody who isn't family and wouldn't feel obligated to do so.

But I'm desperate for confirmation from Marissa and to have everything settled.

"You haven't dated for very long," Courtney says. "You think she's ready?"

Marissa has to be ready, right?

By this time tomorrow, she'll have my ring on her finger and we can start planning our future together. It's what I need.

And it will be perfect.

"Hey, Marissa. It's time to get up."

"I'm sleeping," I mutter.

"I have a surprise for you," Vince says.

Hmm. A surprise. Could be nice.

But you know what's really nice? Sleep. I pull the blankets up to my chin.

He sighs. "Humor me and get out of bed."

"Fine, fine."

When I stay motionless under the covers, he lifts me up and sets me on my feet.

"Soon I'll be too big for you to do that," I say.

"I'm sure I'll manage."

I look at the clock. "It's not even seven, and it's Saturday."

"I'm aware. But what if I'm bringing you to a cheesecake buffet?"

This is a good point. Probably not true because if so, he's just ruined the surprise. But perhaps it's something equally good.

I get dressed and curse the fact that pregnancy doesn't allow me to start my day with three cups of coffee.

We're out the door ten minutes later without eating breakfast, but Vince is carrying a picnic basket, so apparently food is coming with us.

Good. I used to skip breakfast sometimes, but no longer.

A car is waiting for us outside his building, and it takes us west, dropping us off on Parkside Drive.

We walk into High Park. It's a little chilly at this hour, but Vince puts his arm around me and it's not so bad. I haven't been here in years. We pass the adventure playground, which reminds me of a castle, and I imagine him catching our child at the bottom of the slide.

Next, we pass cherry trees at peak bloom.

Ah. That's why we're here. To see the cherry blossoms before the park gets busy. A few people are walking their dogs or jogging, but it's not crowded.

Yeah, okay, maybe it was worth waking up for this, even if the sky is a little gray.

We're approaching the pond when Vince stops walking and puts down the picnic basket.

"I want to take a picture of you," he says. "You're pregnant and cute, remember."

I make a show of rolling my eyes, but I pose beside a cherry tree and hope I can smile properly at this time on a Saturday morning without any coffee.

But I'm with Vince, standing under a blossoming tree, and it's kind of magical here.

And then he gets down on one knee, and I freeze.

Oh, no.

He pulls something small out of his pocket. I know exactly what it is.

Sure enough, he opens up a velvet box, revealing a ring. It's white gold or platinum, with a sensibly-sized diamond. It's just the sort of engagement ring I'd want.

And it scares the crap out of me.

"Marissa Chan," he says, smiling up at me, "will you

marry me?"

This time, I know he's not joking.

This time, I don't kick him in the shin.

I cover my mouth with my hand, and I shake my head.

"Marissa?" he says.

Perhaps he thinks I'm overcome with joy.

I slip to the ground, and I keep shaking my head.

He reaches out to steady me. "Marissa?"

"No," I whisper. "I can't."

"Why not? I love you. I want to spend my life with you." He's all earnestness now, and I hate it.

"We haven't been together for long."

"But I know what I want. And we're having a baby together."

"Yes, goddammit, I'm aware of that. Nobody is more aware of that than me."

"Do you love me?" he asks.

"I've loved many men, but I didn't marry any of them."

"Do you love me?"

I shut my eyes. I can't bear to look at him now. "No."

We're quiet for one long, horrible moment.

Then I open my eyes, and he says, "You act like you love me."

"I care for you. I know you'll be a good dad. But I can't marry a man I don't love. Put that goddamn ring away."

Finally, he snaps the box shut and stows it back in his pocket.

"I've never felt this way before, Marissa."

"I believe you love me, but I still feel like you're desperate for me to save you. For me to give you this idyllic family life that you think will complete you. But it's not going to be idyllic."

"Look, I know there will be sleepless nights and utter exhaustion and piles of poopy diapers, but it will all be wonderful because I'm doing it with you."

"It's too much pressure. Being the center of Vince Fong's universe. Being responsible for your fulfillment. What person could deal with that?"

"You don't have to do anything special. You just have to be you."

"It still doesn't change the fact that I don't love you."

He turns away from me. "*Dammit.*"

I've never heard him angry like this before. Anger is just not part of who Vince is, and yet I'm doing this to him.

I wish I could say yes. Oh, I do.

But I can't.

Something is holding me back from loving him. And besides, there's the pressure. The whirlwind of this whole thing.

I just cannot. The thought of having that ring on my finger makes me cold. My life has changed so much lately. The baby is enough for now.

"I know why you can't love me." His voice has an unfamiliar edge to it. "Why I'll never be good enough."

"Vince, you're—"

"Because I'll never be as perfect as your father. The version of him that you've created in your head. Nobody can compete with that."

"No! That's not true."

His eyes are hard stone. Me, I'm trying not to burst into tears. Stupid hormones.

"You've had lots of relationships, but you've never been engaged. Why? It's not because you don't believe in marriage. It's not because you were waiting for me, the man whose baby you're carrying."

"You act like that means something, other than a freaky failure of birth control."

"I think it does."

"It can't."

"So why have you never been engaged?" he presses.

"I just didn't love them enough!"

"And why can't you love me even a little?"

I shake my head. "I don't know. Why do you keep pushing

me? I won't marry you, I wish I could, but I can't. Isn't that enough of an answer? Why do you want to make me feel more broken?"

I really don't want to cry, but I do.

I never used to think I was broken. Sure, I hadn't found a partner, but that didn't mean there was anything wrong with me, right? Just bad luck, like my father's accident.

Now, I can't stop crying, because I can't help thinking I'm too broken to be a good mother, and what if I can't even love my child?

"Oh, shit," he murmurs. "Can I hug you? Will you let me?"

I nod, because even though I'm pissed at him for putting me in this position, I do like him. I find his presence comforting.

"I have food." Vince opens up the basket. "Do you want anything?" He pulls out fruit salad, rolls, and bakeapple jam. There are wraps with spinach and cheese. There's even a mini matcha double fromage cheesecake, plus a thermos with tea. He pours me a small cup.

I immediately put it to my lips and burn my tongue, but it doesn't hurt as much as it should. Then I grab a wrap and stuff it inelegantly in my mouth before I start wolfing down the cheesecake.

Vince watches me with an unreadable expression. He wants something I can't give him, and I feel awful. It breaks my heart, quite frankly.

If it hurts so much, does that mean I love him?

No, I don't think it does.

Maybe he's right, and I see my dad as a superhero that no one will ever live up to.

No, I don't think that's quite right, either.

I'm mad at him for pushing me. How long has it been since he proposed the first time? Three or four months? That's not enough time for me to change my mind.

But maybe it should be.

I've had lots of experience, and I know myself well. We've gotten quite close. He's a good person.

Is it unreasonable for me to feel like he should have something more in his life, other than me? To feel like it's too much pressure?

I have no idea anymore.

I feel like we're breaking each other.

And yet, we're having this baby.

I stop eating and put my arms around him. I want to hug him and kick him in the shin at the same time. My thoughts are a jumble. Another person might be elated right now, yet here I am, a quivering mess.

"You shouldn't have asked me," I tell him.

"I can see that now," he says mildly.

"I wasn't ready."

"When will you be ready?"

"I don't know."

He sighs. "I'm sorry. I really am."

"I know you are. I know you don't want to hurt me."

"Of course not. I would never."

He doesn't take back what he said about my father, though.

"Do you want to keep dating?" he asks. "Or is this over?"

I pretend I don't hear how his voice is shaking. "I'm not sure. Give me a week, okay? I'll see you at the ultrasound on Friday, and I'm sure I'll have figured everything out by then."

At least, I hope I will.

"Alright," he says. "I'll help you home now?"

"No, I'll stay here for a while."

"I'll make sure there's a car waiting for you where we entered the park."

I want to protest, but I don't have the energy. It's Saturday morning, and I've already had a proposal, but no coffee.

I sit there for another ten minutes after he leaves, keeping my mind as blank as I can. Then I get up and head back, under the fluttering blossoms.

~

I don't go home. I have the car take me straight to my mom's.

When Larry opens the door, I throw my arms around him. He's the closest thing I have to a father now. He hugs me back, somewhat awkwardly—this isn't the sort of relationship we have, and maybe that's my fault, maybe I haven't tried hard enough with him and his children. I was so used to it being just me and my mom, but I have more family now.

After a few seconds, he calls for my mother, and she comes up from the basement.

"Marissa!" she says. "What happened? Is the baby okay?"

"Baby is fine," I say, relieved this much is true. "Vince proposed to me again."

She doesn't need to ask what happened. It doesn't take strong powers of observation to see that I am not happily presenting a ring.

I know she would have liked us to be together, but she doesn't tell me that I'm an idiot for rejecting a rich, well-connected, handsome man who's good to me.

For some reason, I think of Pearl's mom, who definitely would have said that, who would have been horrified if Pearl had gotten pregnant outside of marriage. Pearl's mother has been dead for over a decade, and yes, they had a complicated relationship, but my friend would have given anything for her mother to be a nuisance when planning her wedding, when pregnant with her two children.

Why is life so complicated?

My mom hugs me for a long time, the one person who's always, always been there for me, even when I screamed at her for singing lullabies to me. Even when I told her that *Dad* would have let me go to the mall. Even when I was fifteen and asked her why the fuck she'd wanted Cheetos, because if she hadn't, he would still be here. Every now and then, I said something truly awful, as I bet most teenagers do, and she still loved me.

And now I know, with startling clarity, that I shouldn't worry about loving my child. That I will love them no matter what. That I learned from her, and it will be okay.

I know sometimes mothers have trouble bonding with their babies. You're expected to feel an immediate, everlasting bond when they put the baby on your chest, but not everyone experiences that, and I can't say exactly what will happen in those first couple months. Maybe it will take some time, but I know I will come to love my child.

Vince, though. He'll be there, of course, teaching our baby about coding and rocket science and singing to them in Cantonese even if he doesn't understand the words.

I sniffle into my mother's shirt, and she says something eminently sensible.

"Let's go out for dim sum."

When I was a kid, this was our big treat. I would walk past the restaurants near our Agincourt apartment and see other families, bigger than two people, eating and laughing and arguing. But Mom and I, we would only go out a few times a year, because she was counting her pennies—back when we still had pennies in Canada—to pay the hydro and phone bills.

Still, sometimes we would go out, and it would be A Big Deal.

Now, we're lucky. We can't afford penthouses and the fanciest restaurants and vacations, but we don't need that. We can go out for dim sum—and not at the cheap place—every week and stuff ourselves silly, and at one point, that would have been an unthinkable luxury.

I ate an hour ago, but whatever, I'm pregnant and hungry.

I manage a wobbly smile. "Yes, let's have dim sum."

[27]

VINCE

WHEN I LEAVE HIGH PARK, the ring still in my pocket, I get a call from my real estate agent. There's a new house on the market, and I have the cab driver take me to Yonge and Lawrence to see it.

It's exactly what I want.

I push aside the images that bombard my brain as I walk through the house. Images of Marissa and Baby at different ages.

Instead, I try to focus on what's here. The immaculate house, everything arranged just so, probably by a staging company.

Afterward, I go back home, and I think about texting Brian. That's what I used to do when I was feeling down. We wouldn't talk about anything important, but we'd go out and have fun. Though for most of the past few years, I wouldn't have been awake at this time on a Saturday.

I wonder if he's awake.

It doesn't matter. The last person who needs to deal with my broken heart is Brian. Besides, I don't actually want to go anywhere.

I head to my living room and take out a bottle of whiskey, but then I put it back.

Instead, I sit vacantly on my couch and stare at the black screen of my enormous TV, feeling utterly useless.

She said no.

I'd been convinced that everything would be perfect. She'd say yes, and we'd feed each other cheesecake beneath the blossoms and try not to jump each other…and sometime before Baby came, we'd have a small wedding and move into a house together. Somewhere conveniently located for our families and her job. Decent-sized, but not huge and showy. Baby would come, and we'd spend the first year looking after our child together, and then she'd go back to work and I'd stay home.

I had it all mapped out. It seemed so real—and so close. Like I could reach out and touch it. Sure, she'd never said she loved me, but it felt like she did, even if she couldn't say the words.

I didn't think she'd turn me down. Again.

Am I right about her father?

I don't know, but what does it matter.

A no is a no.

And I hurt her.

I don't fully understand it, but I did. That's my own damn fault, for not knowing shit-all about relationships.

I lie down on my couch, curled up in a ball. I put my hands to my chest, like I'm trying to reach my heart and ease the pain.

Of course, my heart is inside my fucking body and I cannot just reach inside and take it out and if I did it would kill me and I think I saw something like that on *Once Upon a Time*? One of those shows I binge-watched when I had nothing better to do.

My phone buzzes. Holden is in town for the weekend.

I tell him I'm not up for it.

I continue to lie there, for I don't know how long, and wonder what Marissa is doing.

I hope she's not crying anymore.

~

"What the hell is wrong with you?"

When I wake up, the weirdest thing is happening.

Someone is taking off my shoes.

I open my eyes and am relieved to see it's Brian.

"How did you get in?" I ask.

"Uh, you left the door unlocked?"

"Why are you here?"

"Holden texted me, worried when you said you weren't up for seeing him this weekend."

"And why are you taking off my shoes?" I ask as he sets the second one on the floor.

"Because it offends me, as an Asian and a Canadian, to see you wearing shoes indoors. When you're sleeping on your couch, no less." He shudders.

"Fair point."

"What happened?"

"I asked her to marry me, she said no."

It's completely unfair for him to have to remove my shoes and listen to me moan about my heartbreak.

Somebody loves me, but it's not the person I want.

"You don't need to be here," I say. "I'm perfectly fine. Haven't even drunk any alcohol."

"You shouldn't be alone right now."

"Touching, but… You know I'm not going to change my mind about you."

"I know," Brian says, slightly annoyed, "but as your friend, I don't think you should be alone. You look like shit."

"Thanks for the compliment."

"Cut the sarcasm and tell me who to call for you."

"My grandmother."

"Very funny," he says. "I know that's the last thing you want."

"My brothers."

"Alright. I can do that."

"Thank you," I mumble before drifting back to sleep.

~

"General Bloopy says good morning!"

This time, I wake up to a stuffed purple dinosaur nuzzling my nose.

I sit up and rub my eyes. It's dark outside.

"What time is it?" I ask.

"It's time to wake up and touch your toes!" General Bloopy speaks in an annoying, singsong voice. He dips his head to touch his left front foot, then his right front foot.

"Oh, fuck off," I mutter.

General Bloopy gasps. "Such shocking language! Somebody needs a snuggle."

The dinosaur then, uh, vigorously snuggles me as only a bloopisaurus can.

On the other side of the room, someone cracks up with laughter. It's Cedric.

Julian is the one manipulating General Bloopy into saying completely out-of-character things, believe it or not.

"You seem to think I'm Evie," I say, "rather than a grown-ass man."

He shrugs. "Now you know how I feel when you piss me off."

Perhaps he has a point.

"So you're sleeping at eight thirty in the evening," Cedric says as he sits down in a recliner. "This is what happens when you get dumped?"

"To be clear," I say, "I didn't get dumped. She simply refused my proposal and decided she didn't want to see me for a week."

"So you're still together?"

"Maybe? I don't know."

"Seems like it might not be all that bad, then."

"She has no idea when she'll be ready, and Baby will be coming this fall."

"That's many months away," Julian points out, in irritating older-brother fashion.

"You call you child 'Baby'?" Cedric asks.

"We don't know their name," I say. "What am I supposed to call them? Fetus? Goji berry? What did you call Evie, Julian?"

"Bean," he says, "but 'Baby' is sensible. Like how Holly Golightly in *Breakfast at Tiffany's* refused to name her cat, just called him 'Cat.'"

"But we'll name Baby eventually. Just not until they're born."

"I've still never seen *Breakfast at Tiffany's*," Cedric says. "Remember how Mom wouldn't let us watch it?"

Julian nods. "Because of Mickey Rooney. A white guy, playing a horrible stereotype of an Asian man. And yeah, it was that bad. But we're getting wildly off topic. We're here because Vince looks like shit after Marissa refused his proposal. I admit I was surprised she said no, but Courtney wasn't."

Ugh. I should have listened to Courtney.

"Stop being melodramatic and acting like it's the end of the world," Julian says.

"Me?" I say. "Melodramatic? Well, I never!"

He shakes his head and puts his hand to his temple. I think I've given him many headaches over the years.

"Wait a week, like she asked," Julian continues, "then see what she says."

"A week feels like forever," I groan.

"The melodrama. Save me."

"She said she doesn't love me. I told her it was because I'd never be able to live up to the image of her dad she'd created in her mind. She started crying."

"Look, I understand being entirely sure about someone, even when it hasn't been very long. But it really hasn't been long, and maybe it takes her time to fall in love. Hopefully she'll give you more time, and then you can be there for her. Be patient."

"We're having a baby together."

"You don't need to have everything perfectly arranged by then."

"I don't think you'd cope well with that," I tell Julian.

"You may be right. But you love Marissa. Think about what she needs, not what you need, and find something to do with your time rather than obsessing about this."

"You know I won't be able to help that."

"But still. Try. Don't just sleep and play videogames all day."

"Marissa says I need to find something to do with my life, other than being a parent. Not a career like what I had before. Just…something."

"Marissa has a point."

"Yes," Cedric says, "I agree."

"She feels like being the center of my universe is too much pressure."

"Well," Julian says, "I'm sure she'll be the center of your universe, but it's healthy to have multiple interests, and you've told me before that you're bored. So, find something."

"As if it's that easy." I try to sit up, but my body hurts. My mind hurts. I lie back down. "She suggested the TCCC, but other than giving money, there's only so much I can do without speaking any useful language."

"You could learn."

"Yeah, thank you, Mr. I-speak-five-languages-fluently."

"Six."

"Whatever. I'm utter shit at languages, as you know."

My stomach growls. I haven't eaten anything since this morning, under that blasted blooming cherry tree.

"Let's order some food," Cedric suggests. "Yang's Dumplings?"

"No. Not that."

"How can you not be in the mood for dumplings?"

"I'm not in the mood for anything."

"Vince," Julian says sternly.

"Marissa and I had Yang's Dumplings together. Let's have pizza instead."

Then I remember that first weekend, when we ate cold pizza.

Fuck it. I have to eat something. Pizza it is.

"Oh, by the way," Julian says, after he places the order. "Dad had Marissa investigated."

"Jesus Christ. I didn't want him to do that. I hope nobody was following her." I hate the thought of her privacy being invaded.

"Well, it's over now, and he's convinced she isn't angling for all your money. So he's not against this anymore."

"Perfect timing."

"Vince, this will work out. It's not going exactly the way you wish, but you have to accept that the world won't always bend to your will, as hard as that may be for you. Just...be there for her in the way she wants. Give her space when she needs it. I suspect that finding herself unexpectedly pregnant has brought up a lot of things for her, and you might not feel like you're rushing into this, but she does, and that's okay. And she's the one who's pregnant, not you. She trusts you, right?"

"Yeah, she does."

"I do, too," Julian says. "Even if there were years when you were constantly talking about hookers and blow, and I could never be sure what was real and what was a joke."

Apparently our conversation has gotten too heavy for him, because he pulls out General Bloopy again.

"I love you, Vince!" the bloopisaurus says. "I'm sure you'll make a great dad." He plants a kiss on my cheek.

"Julian, man, I think you're losing it," Cedric says.

"Evie refused to sleep last night."

Our pizza arrives, and I confiscate General Bloopy from Julian. I start feeling a little less like complete shit, which is an improvement.

What else could I do with my life?

It's terrifying, yeah, but a little exciting at the same time.

~

Unfortunately, after spending most of Saturday sleeping on the couch, I have a terrible night's sleep. I suppose I should get used to this for when the baby comes.

After coffee and cold pizza for Sunday breakfast, I stumble into the room full of things for Baby and look around. I can't wait to meet Baby.

And God, I miss Marissa. And I will keep missing her. But I will keep my mind on the ultrasound at the end of this week, when I'll see her next.

She might not love me now, but that doesn't mean she never will.

I refuse to let everything go to shit. I remember burning out and how badly I coped with it. Now, I'm going to create a balanced life that will not destroy my mental health.

It doesn't sound glamorous, but I don't need that anymore.

My gaze falls on *Baby Loves Coding!* and it gives me an idea.

MARISSA

I'M in the waiting room. My ultrasound is in twenty minutes, and Vince isn't here yet, but that's okay. There's still time, and I know he'll be here soon. Usually he picks me up for my appointments, but this one is at the end of the day, and he was going to visit his niece first and asked if he could meet me here instead.

I've thought about Vince a lot in the past week, and I think I want to keep seeing him. Maybe I'll come to love him, and it's just not something I can do quickly.

That doesn't mean I'm broken.

He's able to fully commit to things in a short period of time, and I admire that about him. It's not me, though, and that's okay. He just has to understand.

Still, something bothers me.

He said I couldn't love him because he couldn't live up to the superhero dad of my imagination. I suspect he regrets it. I know he feels terrible about hurting me. I know he'll listen to what I have to say today.

But I can't help wondering if there's an element of truth to it.

Yes, my dad was a bit of a superhero in my mind. Perhaps,

although I didn't grow up with any important adult men in my life, that's why I had high expectations of the men I dated.

Except I didn't really have high expectations, did I? I just expected to be treated decently, and the fact that some people might see that as unrealistic is sad.

I don't think Vince is right, but it still bothers me.

Sitting across from me is a woman, about my age, who looks very pregnant. She's here alone, but she's got a ring on her finger. We smile at each other.

The last time I had an ultrasound, I was suffering from morning sickness and puked in the garbage can when the couple nearby called Everclear "classic rock."

That was seven weeks ago. A lot has happened in seven weeks.

Just then, I experience a strange fluttery feeling.

I grin. I think I just felt Baby move for the first time!

Oh, I wish Vince was here. I send him a text.

I wait a few minutes, but he doesn't reply. He's probably driving. He'll be here soon.

Baby is apparently now the size of a mango or tomato. Last week, they were the size of a pepper. Honestly, a tomato is a terrible basis for comparison. Tomatoes vary a lot in size, don't they? And I'm not talking grape or cherry tomatoes—I know that's not what they mean—but all the others. Aren't they often smaller than peppers?

Hell, maybe mangoes vary a lot, too. There's just not a lot of variety in mangoes at my local grocery store.

This reminds me of my conversation with Vince about limes and plums.

God, where is he?

It's less than five minutes until my appointment time.

A few months ago, I wouldn't have been surprised. I would have chalked it up to him being Vince Fong, the playboy who somehow managed to knock me up. The guy who'd be the fun father, showing up a couple times a month to take our kid out for ice cream and play catch.

But I know him better now, and this isn't like him.

I send him another text. *Where are you??*

Surely he should be out of his car by now, right? Hurrying from his parking spot to the ultrasound clinic?

He's going to be late. It's not like Vince to be late and not tell me anything.

In fact, it's really not like him at all.

Whenever I have an appointment or an unbearable craving for cheesecake, he's a hundred percent committed. Even when Cheese & Me was sold out of matcha double fromage cheesecake, he didn't give up. He got me what I wanted.

Sure, things are a little awkward between us now, but he loves me. He loves Baby. He would be here no matter what.

One minute.

He would be here no matter what.

Unless…

My blood runs cold.

I put my hands on my stomach to comfort Baby, even though there's nothing I can do to comfort myself.

Something terrible must have happened. That's the only explanation.

My dad went to get a bag of Cheetos for my mother, and he never came back.

When I met up with Vince after discovering I was pregnant, I was thrilled I'd be able to give my child a father, the father I didn't have, even if he wasn't exactly the one I would have chosen.

Except now I think Vince will be the best father possible for Baby.

And the truth is, I did have a father when I was nothing more than a mango-sized fetus in my mom's uterus. Maybe he talked to me. Maybe she placed his hand on her stomach so he could feel me kick.

He held me, he changed my diapers, he played with me.

He sang to me.

I had a father for three years.

He was younger than Vince when he died.

It suddenly seems ridiculous that I haven't worried about anything happening to Vince, and now he's not here when he's supposed to be.

It's all wrong.

Oh, God. Baby isn't going to know their father at all. Baby won't even have a hazy memory of their dad singing them a Cantonese lullaby.

No, this can't be happening.

And maybe it isn't. Maybe there's a perfectly reasonable explanation...except I can't wrap my mind around that. If he couldn't be here, Vince would have contacted me some way or another. If his phone was dead, he would have grabbed a phone off a random passerby and punched in my number—I'm sure he has my number memorized.

"Are you okay?"

I blink and realize I'm crying.

"Are you okay?" the woman across from me asks again.

"Yeah," I say, even though it's clearly a lie, but she lets it go.

He's three minutes late now, and I'm just thankful they haven't called me in yet. We're supposed to find out if it's a boy or girl today.

Now it will just be me finding out.

How is this happening?

I never even got to tell Vince that I love him.

It hits me now, overwhelming in its intensity.

I do love him.

And I understand why I couldn't tell him, why I couldn't

acknowledge it to myself. It had nothing to do with him not living up to my father.

It's because I'm absolutely terrified of losing someone I love.

But why could I say "I love you" to boyfriends in the past? Perhaps, deep down, I knew they weren't right for me, and that made it easier.

Vince, however, is the guy for me.

Admitting I loved him would be admitting how much it would hurt when he was gone. Nearly every memory I have is of the *after*, my father's funeral being the first memory I could recall for the longest time. It's still much clearer than my memory of that song.

Grief was a part of my early childhood. I don't remember screaming when my mom sang to me instead of my dad, but it happened.

I do remember watching my mother grapple with his absence.

On the rare occasions we went out for dim sum, I couldn't help wishing he were there.

I've built a life I'm proud of. I didn't think of my father a lot in the last ten years...until I got pregnant, which made me think more about my own childhood and what I wanted to be different for my son or daughter.

I know a child's early years are so important. I had a loving family, but I was affected by loss in ways I didn't fully compre-hend, and I was desperate to avoid going through that again, even if I wasn't consciously aware of it.

I met Vince right after I learned my mom's tumor was benign. I couldn't bear the thought of that loss, and not allowing myself to admit my love for him was a form of self-preservation.

Shit. I'm an idiot. Why couldn't I have understood all this before?

Why couldn't I have said "I love you" before it was too late?

Because knowing I love him...it doesn't make me want to run away, even if it's scary. My subconscious might be trying to protect me, but I know that having something wonderful involves some level of risk, and he's worth the risk.

Or *was* worth it.

There's an annoying crunching sound coming from the other side of the room. A man is eating Cheetos. Are you even supposed to eat in the waiting room?

I want to confront him, but I force myself to stay in my seat and keep my mouth shut.

Once again, I check my phone, just in case.

Nothing. Still nothing.

I was right. Something awful has happened. He's gone and I never got to tell him…

I said I hated the pressure of feeling like the center of his life, of him building everything around me and Baby. I wish—

"Marissa Chan?" The receptionist is standing in front of me. "It's time for your ultrasound."

"I…can't," I stammer. "My husband. He's not here."

I call him my husband because I wish it were true.

Seeing my distress, she says, "I'm sure he's coming soon."

I shake my head.

"Well, the person after you is already here. She could go first?"

When I nod, the receptionist leads the pregnant woman across from me toward the back. They give me sympathetic smiles.

The Cheetos man keeps chewing.

Vince still isn't here.

I'm thinking of him as though he's dead and alive at the same time.

Was it a car accident?

It was probably a car accident.

Baby and I are going to be alone, just like Mom and I were alone.

Except I'm in a better financial position. I have my mother, too. Larry and his family. I have my friends. I have Vince's family.

Did Vince rewrite his will to leave money for me?

I don't care about that. I just want *him*. I want him to hold me and take me out for mocktails and look at me as though I'm beautiful, even when I feel anything but.

I want to be under that cherry tree again. I want a chance to do it over and say yes.

As I trace my bare ring finger, a wave of grief overtakes me. I clutch my stomach and bend over, but I can't cry anymore. It's too horrible to cry.

I'm making a scene, and I hate making a scene.

I consider calling my mother, but I can't stand the thought of telling her all this. Pearl is probably picking up her kids from daycare.

Carrie. I'll call Carrie.

Before I do, though, I try calling Vince. It immediately goes to voicemail, and the sound of his voice causes a painful knot in my chest.

Then I call my friend.

"I'm at the ultrasound clinic," I say.

"Is something wrong with the baby?" she asks. Because I must sound terrible, and I'm calling rather than texting.

"No, but Vince isn't here. He's really late and not answering his phone. I think something bad happened. He never breaks his promises. I think..." I can't even say it. "My dad went to the convenience store and he never came back and I can't deal with that again. Vince proposed to me on Saturday and I said no and..."

She doesn't tell me I'm being stupid. "I'm going to get an Uber. I'll come to you, okay?"

Carrie is my friend for going out and having fun. For taking me to house parties where I make out with handsome strangers.

Still, I know I can count on her.

"Okay," I say. "I'll text you the location."

I end the call and close my eyes. Maybe this will be okay. Carrie is coming. I won't be alone. But Vince…

I keep clutching my stomach. I'd forsake dim sum and cheesecake for the rest of my life if only I could see him again.

Vince, I love you so much.

"Marissa."

[29]

MARISSA

I open my eyes cautiously, afraid to hope.

Vince is kneeling before me.

I reach out tentatively and pat his arm. He's real. He's not a ghost.

"You're here," I say, launching myself at him.

"I'm here. I'm so sorry I'm late."

"I love you." I have to say that before anything else. "I love you and I'm sorry I didn't realize it before but I do."

"I love you, too," he murmurs, his arms coming around me.

"I thought you were dead and I'd never get to tell you."

It sounds foolish now. He was less than fifteen minutes late, and I totally lost my shit and assumed the worst-case scenario.

"You thought…like your dad," he whispers.

I nod.

"Oh, no." His voice breaks and he hugs me tight. "I knew you'd worry, but I didn't think you'd assume—"

"Because you're always here. And then you weren't."

He lifts me back into my chair and sits beside me. "Evie had a high fever and was really fussy. She'd never been like this before, and Courtney was very worried and not coping well with it. She managed to make a last-minute appointment with Evie's doctor and wanted me to go with her, since I was around and Julian is out of town for work. Afterward, I ran to my car and pulled out my phone to call you, and the battery was dead. I thought I'd be able to get here in time if I left right away, so I didn't look for a charger. Then traffic was terrible and I couldn't find a parking spot until after your appointment time. Did you have the ultrasound?"

"Not yet. They switched my appointment with someone else's." I feel the need to say something light. "Did you know Baby is now as big as a mango? I felt them move for the first time today! Or possibly it was gas." I can't laugh, but I want to make him laugh, and he does chuckle. Then I fully register his why-I-was-late story. "Is Evie okay?"

"She has an ear infection. She'll be fine. Oh, Marissa, I can't believe I didn't charge my phone. Dammit. I'm usually better about that. And I'm so sorry about some of the things I said to you on Saturday."

"It's okay," I say. "You were wrong"—he laughs at this—"but I understand why you thought that. Yes, I'll marry you, Vince. I want to wear your ring." I touch the empty space on my ring finger.

"You don't need to. I understand, I was pushing you."

"But it's what I want. When I said I couldn't love you, couldn't marry you, I was protecting myself, afraid of losing someone again. I didn't realize what I was doing, but when I thought I lost you…" I release a choked sob. "It hurt so much, even though I'd never told you how I felt."

"I'm so sorry," he says again.

"There are never any guarantees, but I know I can't live life being afraid. If I'd been aware of what I was doing, I would have stopped myself from doing it." I start patting his pockets, trying to find the ring.

He knows what I'm doing, and he laughs softly. "It's at home. I'll get it for you tonight."

"I shouldn't have told you that you need to find something else to do with your life right away. Yes, knowing you, you need something just for yourself, but I could have helped you figure it out. It's not that big of a deal and—"

"No, you were right," he says, "and I know what I'm going to do."

"Do you?"

"I want to teach kids about coding. At first I thought I'd start my own organization, but I don't need to start everything on my own. There are already places doing what I want to do, and there's one that's happy to have me work with them and take my money."

"I think you'll be great at it." I hug him tightly. I don't want to let go. Some part of me is still afraid he'll evaporate into thin air.

"You know," he whispers, "I used to worry that no one would love me, but now…"

Oh. I can imagine Vince feeling that way, beneath his swagger. Sure, he acts cocky, but it's kind of for show. And I told him repeatedly how I didn't love him—that must have felt like confirmation of his fears. My heart twists.

"I'm here for you," I say, pressing a kiss to his cheek. "No matter what."

"Marissa?"

I see Carrie over Vince's shoulder.

She comes over to us. "You got here after all," she says to Vince.

"Yeah."

She turns to me. "Do you need to me kick his ass?"

"No, no. Everything's okay."

She smiles at me, and crap, I made her come all this way and I don't need her here now. In fact, I'd rather spend the time with Vince.

She heads back toward the door.

"I'm sorry," I tell her. There have been a lot of *sorry*s lately.

"It's fine. There's an accessories shop nearby that I've been meaning to check out, but I rarely make it this far north."

Yeah, Carrie is one of those people who usually stay south of Bloor.

She waves at me, and then it's just me and Vince again.

Well, the two of us and everyone else in the waiting room.

"It's time for your ultrasound," the receptionist says to me. "Are you ready?"

"Yes," I say, "I'm ready."

Everything is fine with Baby, as far as the ultrasound technician can tell, but she'll send the results to my doctor. She asks if we want to know if it's a boy or a girl, and we nod.

"It's a boy," she says.

"Oh!" If anything, I had imagined Baby being a girl, but I don't care.

Vince takes my hand and squeezes.

We're having a boy together!

After the ultrasound, we go to my condo, where I pick up a few things for the weekend, then get back in Vince's car so we can head down to his place.

"Actually," he says as he fastens his seatbelt, "let's make a detour first."

To my surprise, we drive north.

"Is this a fancy new cheesecake place?" I ask.

"It has nothing to do with food. Shocking, I know."

We turn onto a residential street, and he puts the car in park.

"See that house?" He points across the street.

It's a new-ish stone house. Though many of the homes on the street are older brick houses, this one looks like it was built in the past decade, and it's a little bigger, but not too big. We're maybe a five- or ten-minute walk from Yonge and Lawrence.

I have a sneaking suspicion…

"You want to buy it?" I ask, noting the sign in front of the house.

"I did buy it."

Right. I see now that the sign says "sold."

"I would have asked you to look at it with me," he says, "but you'd just…you know. Plus I had to act fast. I thought I could give it to you, if you were willing to accept it, or I'd live in it myself. But now, I'm hoping—"

"Yes." I throw my arms around him. "Yes. It looks perfect, and it's not too far from the office or your family. Or too long of a drive from my mom's."

"That was the point."

Of course it was. Of course he was thinking of that.

"I get to decorate it," I say. "Your penthouse is nice and all, but I don't want our house to look like a swanky bachelor pad."

"I don't want that, either."

I cup his cheeks, and as I kiss him, I remember the first kiss we shared all those months ago, before he even knew my name. When I met him at that party, I never would have imagined that several months later, we would find ourselves here.

In love. A baby on the way.

Sitting in front of the house we'll live in together.

All of this flits through my mind, but then I get lost in his kiss. His lips on mine, his arms holding me close, despite the awkward position in the car.

He brushes his cheek against mine. "I love you."

"I love you, too."

I can say it now without hesitation.

~

The next evening, we go out for dinner. I'm craving poutine, so we head to a bistro with excellent duck confit poutine—after checking online that cheese curds are pasteurized and safe for pregnant people—and then to Cheese & Me, where we buy the very last matcha double fromage cheesecake.

And then I decide I've eaten enough food for the day, and we return to Vince's penthouse and make extremely good use of his large bed.

Afterward, we lie in bed together, my head on his chest. I twist the ring on my finger.

We told our families about the engagement earlier. They were all very excited. His grandmother wanted to come over immediately to congratulate us in person, but eventually he managed to put her off and promised to visit his family tomorrow. Julian has returned from his business trip, and Evie is doing much better now.

Suddenly, there's a flutter in my belly. Just like yesterday.

"Oh, it's Baby!" I say. "He's moving."

Vince puts his hand on my increasing belly.

"I feel him," he says, wonder in his voice.

His face close to my stomach, Vince softly sings the lullaby that my father used to sing to me. He's learned the words, though I'm not sure he knows what they mean.

I wipe my eyes. The past several months have been an emotional roller coaster, but I love what I have now.

I hold Vince close and grin the goofiest grin ever.

[EPILOGUE]
VINCE

The following January...

"Baby!" Evie shrieks, running into the room. "Baby!"

Julian scoops her off her feet just before she pokes Baby's face. "Baby is trying to sleep, Evie. He doesn't want to play with you right now."

Evie glares at her father but allows herself to be taken out of the room. To be spoiled by her grandparents, most likely. We're at Mom and Dad's house for dinner.

Baby has a name now. It's Lucas.

Lucas gurgles from the car seat on the floor, and I *beep* his nose.

He doesn't laugh, but maybe he will tomorrow. He's pretty fickle. One minute he loves General Bloopy, the next minute the dinosaur makes him scream. One day he sleeps through the night, and the next night…

Oh, who am I kidding. Lucas is a terrible sleeper.

He also screams when he has a bath. He's not fickle about that; no, he's quite decisive in his hatred of baths.

Mom says he's exactly like me.

Marissa and I love him dearly, even though we're both exhausted.

When Lucas shuts his eyes, Marissa curls up on the couch and does the same, and I wrap my arms around her.

"You know," I say, "this might be the anniversary of the day Lucas was conceived."

"Oh, is it? I've completely lost track of time."

"It's the one-year anniversary of the day I met you, yeah."

"I'm glad I walked up and kissed you."

"Me, too." I touch the rings on her finger.

We've been living together since we got married, a few months before Lucas arrived. I've been teaching kids how to code a couple afternoons a week since September. I never thought I'd enjoy teaching before, but I do.

My life is so different from what it was like a year ago. I don't miss my old world, though I do miss Brian a little. I haven't seen him in a few months, and from what I hear, his life is quite different now, too.

But I don't regret my past. It led me to Marissa, and now I feel more content and fulfilled. And balanced.

Okay, that's a bit of a lie. It's hard for your life to be truly balanced when you have a three-month-old baby, but I feel good about where I am now.

And I get to do it all with Marissa.

I knew what I wanted the minute she told me she was pregnant, but back then, I couldn't truly envision what it would be like, couldn't comprehend the love I would grow to have for her and Lucas.

Lucas opens his eyes briefly to give me a little smile.

Don't tell Julian, but I think he's cuter than Evie, though she's pretty cute, too.

My son closes his eyes again and quickly falls asleep. Perhaps by the time we get home, he'll be wide awake and crying, but for now, it's peaceful.

Marissa is asleep as well, her head resting on my shoulder, her hand feeling up my bicep. I'll let her sleep for a while before we head home, where I have a gift in honor of our anniversary. We've already had dessert at my parents' house, but I bought a little chestnut cake for her, along with a necklace.

Then afterward…

Well, I have some ideas, though if she prefers to snuggle up against my side and sleep, that's okay, too.

My father approaches the little room near the back of the house. He looks at the sleeping baby in the car seat and my sleeping wife draped all over me, and he smiles.

When he leaves, Marissa presses the side of her face against my nose.

"I love you," I murmur, stroking her hair.

She replies with a snore, but that's okay.

I know she loves me and trusts me, and we're going to have a great life together. It won't go exactly as we plan, but it'll be with her, and that's what matters.

Yes, I'm in love, and it's the most wonderful thing in the world.

ACKNOWLEDGMENTS

Thank you to my editor, Latoya C. Smith, for helping me make this book the best it could be, as well as Suleikha Snyder for coming up with the title. The lovely cover was created by Flirtation Designs.

Thank you also to Toronto Romance Writers, plus my husband and father, for all your support, and to my little niece and nephew for providing some of the inspiration for this book.

Jackie Lau decided she wanted to be a writer when she was in grade two, sometime between writing "The Heart That Got Lost" and "The Land of Shapes." She later studied engineering and worked as a geophysicist before turning to writing romance novels. Jackie lives in Toronto with her husband, and despite living in Canada her whole life, she hates winter. When she's not writing, she enjoys gelato, gourmet donuts, cooking, hiking, and reading on the balcony when it's raining.

To learn more and sign up for her newsletter, visit jackielaubooks.com.

Kwan Sisters/Fong Brothers Series

Grumpy Fake Boyfriend

Mr. Hotshot CEO

Pregnant by the Playboy

Holidays with the Wongs Series

A Match Made for Thanksgiving

A Second Chance Road Trip for Christmas

A Fake Girlfriend for Chinese New Year

A Big Surprise for Valentine's Day

Baldwin Village Series

One Bed for Christmas (prequel novella)

The Ultimate Pi Day Party

Ice Cream Lover

Man vs. Durian

Chin-Williams Series

Not Another Family Wedding

He's Not My Boyfriend